Last Wave
by
Earl T. Roske

Thank You:
Tim, Andrew, Erin
Trish, Megan
Andy

For my wife and daughter.
&
Judy, my mom.
20 November 1943 – 14 March 2019

Other Work by Earl T. Roske

01

It was as simple a suicide note as Acharon could imagine. "Got tired of waiting. Sorry." A briefer one might have just said "bye," but it would have lacked any real meaning. Murphy's, on the other hand, said quite a lot.

Acharon examined the note still in his hand. It had been torn from the back of an antique copy of Utopia. The book was still pressed open, a disposable pen resting in the valley of open pages. The note had been held in place by an open, pristine box of 12 gauge, double-ought buckshot shells. A single shell was absent from the box.

From the neat tear in Utopia, to the clearly printed words on the note, to the use of the ammo box to keep the note in place, it had every appearance of having been done with careful deliberateness.

Clearly, this hadn't been some random decision decided on and acted out with haste. Murphy had put thought into his actions. That meant he'd been thinking about this for a while. But how long of a while? Acharon shrugged and released a sigh he'd been holding back. He and Sovelet would never know. Or at least, he would never know.

The note still dangling in his hand, he turned his attention to Murphy's body. Murphy was slumped sideways in the well-worn easy chair he'd dragged along with him when he'd excused himself from the San Francisco enclave. Blood, hair, and brains stained the top left of the back of the chair. More of Murphy had reached out to spread itself across a bookcase full of recently printed copies of classic and famous philosophical works.

Murphy had obsessively printed books from the book machine in the Last Wave warehouse at Oakland's waterfront. Several times he'd stayed overnight, waiting for books to print and bind while Acharon and Sovelet sailed back to their Acharon-made island to sleep. They'd return for him the following morning where he'd be waiting with an overstuffed box of books and a Christmas morning grin on his face.

Now he was dead and the books were ruined, stained with the blood of his memory. Fortunately no one would ever see it or have to clean it.

Acharon put the note back on the end table and set the box of buckshot on top.

Murphy had been the oldest person Acharon had ever known. At 173, he'd been one of the first born in the Last Wave of humanity. Acharon was one of the last two ever born. His wife, Sovelet, was the other. They were only 149, born on the same day. The two youngest people left on Earth.

With a last long look at Murphy, Acharon pulled his homemade two-way radio out of his pocket and pressed the call button.

"Sovie? You available?"

There was a moment of silence which Acharon used to scan the scene one more time. Murphy had sealed the house well. Not a fly buzzed around his open skull, not a single bug crawled and dined on his remains. A well-planned exit.

"Just got out." The voice was scratchy through the speaker of the radio. They'd lost local cellphone reception fifteen years back from an unfortunate lightning strike. No one had expected this kind of accident, so no one had planned for an alternative. Acharon had mentally kicked himself since he'd been part of the advisory committees on product longevity.

With the cell service gone, Acharon had spent a week scouring parts from all over Sausalito and Marin City, taking apart everything from radios and garage door openers to kids' toys until he finally rigged two radios together. They were sturdy and worked over long distances.

"Everything okay?"

Again a long silence.

"Yeah. I'm good."

Sovelet hadn't been feeling herself the last few weeks. She'd been easily winded and tired after their regular everyday activities, always short of breath. She'd tried to put it down to their age but Acharon knew better. With all the advances and preparations made by world governments as the human population wound down to extinction, they were both in better shape and health than a fit fifty-year-old would have been in the early years of the 21st century.

So Acharon had insisted that she go to the medi-pod for an early check-up. As a carrot he told her he'd pop in to visit Murphy, see how he was doing, find out why hadn't he checked in the last few days. Maybe he'd invite Murphy over for dinner. Of course that wasn't happening now.

"How's Murphy?" Sovelet asked. Her voice was rushed and Acharon knew what she was doing. He knew what that meant.

He held his radio up, about to speak, and looked once more at Murphy with his blown-out skull and the shotgun lying between his thighs, the barrel pointing upward. A crooked stick hung in the trigger guard, probably having given Murphy the few extra inches he'd needed to pressure the trigger.

Acharon had given that shotgun to Murphy, along with a rifle and a handgun. All of it was intended to provide protection against the ever-increasing wildlife. There were bears now, roaming the streets of Sausalito. A new meaning to the wild west.

"He's dead," Acharon said after his own hesitation.

"Oh, no. What happened?"

"Hard to say." Acharon began walking through the small house, checking that all the windows were still locked tight. He pulled curtains shut, checked the lock on the back door. "Heart attack. Brain aneurysm. Not sure. He's just dead."

"Well, we're fifty-three, now."

The fifty-three wasn't the population of Sausalito or even California. It was the world population, something that Sovelet had been tracking since she'd graduated from college. Back then they'd just been huge numbers, still in the billions. But as the numbers declined in an almost exponential curve, she began to add names to the numbers. She'd emailed and even talked on the computer with some of them over the past forty years. Now, a little more than fifty were left.

Acharon was never sure of the exact number unless told, but he knew Sovelet always did. In fact, he was pretty sure she knew them all by name and location. Probably had a picture of each of them on her computer.

"He was the oldest," Acharon said. It sounded dumb, but he didn't know what else to say. "Let me just close up the house and I'll be back over to get you."

"You don't want to bury him?"

What was the use of that, Acharon wondered. There used to be reclamation hearses but he hadn't seen one since just before leaving San Francisco.

"No, let's just leave him here. He liked the place and there's no one to bother him."

"What about the animals?"

"I'm locking the place up tight. Should be a long time before even the bugs get to him. He'll probably be mummified by then. It'll be okay, Sovie."

"All right." The hesitant pause again. "Can we go out for dinner?"

As the population decrease continued its inevitable slide to zero, there had been much preparation for the Last Wavers. One of the many inventive constructions was the automated diner. It was unlike those from the 20th century, with everything put into carousel vending machines, cooks working in the background. No, these had been truly automated. Machines opened packages, mixed, stirred, cut and served Michelin star-worthy meals.

As the world's population reached the millions, many of the automated diners, and other systems of convenience, were abandoned by those still alive. When Acharon and Sovelet had left the San Francisco enclave to set up house in Sausalito, Acharon had repaired the local diner. He'd maintained it from that point on and they would have a meal there at least once a month. As long as the packaged and dehydrated food items remained in stock, they'd be able to dine out from time to time.

"Dinner out?"

Usually it was Acharon that had to push for eating at the diner. The meal choices were slim these days, but he liked the idea of going someplace and sitting down for a meal that he, or Sovelet, hadn't prepared. He knew he was being nostalgic. The days of crowded restaurants might be forever gone, but he liked the feel of being out for dinner.

Sovelet suggested dining out only when she wanted to discuss something. Better to have an argument in a neutral place, was her explanation.

"That okay?"

"Sure," Acharon said. "Just wait for me and I'll be right there."

"You do know that I can get there just fine on my own, right?"

"Of course you can. I just like being a gentleman about things."

Without hearing her, he knew she was chuckling. While the experiences were rare, they were both capable of defending themselves against the wildlife. That was the only violent danger now. However, Acharon knew that Sovelet wasn't feeling well, and she might hesitate at the sight of a charging black bear. Better to be safe.

"I'll wait," she finally said. "I'll just sit and read a magazine."

"Mail finally arrive?"

She shared her laugh with him, putting a smile on his face despite the violent mess behind him that had once been Murphy.

"Don't dawdle."

"Be there in a few," Acharon said. He slipped the radio back into his pocket. He went back and considered Murphy.

Murphy had come from the east. From the Miami enclave that had been destroyed by a massive hurricane. He'd told them that most of those that had survived had gone north to Atlanta, Boston, and even New York. He'd taken a different route.

Using the monorail system he'd roamed across the country, staying here or there at other enclaves. Sometimes he'd actually driven a car or hiked out to national monuments or parks. Places that had once seen hundreds of thousands of tourists were now places where the roads were overgrown with brush and grass. Only the animals were left to enjoy the sights.

Murphy had come across to Sausalito after experiencing the fractured community of San Francisco. The enclave in San Francisco had fallen apart for political and personal reasons. Many had remained within the emotionally bitter walls. Others, like Acharon and Sovelet, had chosen to leave. Most had remained within the city, close to the automated amenities. A few had ranged farther, but only Acharon and Sovelet had crossed the bay to the north.

That was where Murphy had found them. They'd welcomed him, glad for the change in routine. They'd offered him space on the barges that Acharon had turned into a floating island. He declined, saying that he wanted some space for himself.

Twenty years he'd lived in the house. He'd tended a small garden and took long walks, often going south to the base of the Golden Gate bridge, its middle span now missing. Sometimes he'd come over for a meal on the island with Acharon and Sovelet. But no matter what he did, he'd always checked in with them every few days.

When he hadn't checked in, and when he hadn't responded to Sovelet's radio call, Acharon had used that as an excuse to get Sovelet to go and sit in the medi-pod for a check-up. It couldn't hurt to just get a check-up was his prod and she'd relented, mostly to get him to check in on Murphy.

Now Murphy was dead and Sovelet wanted to have dinner at the diner. It wasn't turning out to be a good day.

A scratching sound pulled Acharon from his reverie.

He knew the sound and grabbed his shotgun from against the table where he'd leaned it upon seeing Murphy. He stepped quietly across to the front room window and parted the curtains. A coyote was on the porch. It looked around, sniffed the air, and occasionally pawed at the door as if testing it.

Fortunately it was just one of the coyotes and not the wolf pack that had moved into Marin county over the last few decades. With the absence of humans, the other hunters of the world were storming back, sometimes with a vengeance. At Sovelet's request, he'd switched to rock salt and old rubber bullets to annoy and scare away the wolves and coyotes. The bears were a different story.

Instead of shooting the coyote to scare it off, Acharon went to the closet off the living room. He'd made sure that Murphy was stocked to handle intrusions of this sort and had given him several tanks of compressed air attached to truck horns. He pulled one from the closet and hauled it over to the door. He opened the door enough to slide the horn through.

The coyote ran back from the house but turned around in the middle of the grass-covered road to watch the door with suspicion.

Acharon closed the door enough to hold the horn in place, bracing the door with the air tank. With just a brief pause he turned the knob on the tank. The sound of the horn started off soft and low and rose in volume and dipped in pitch until it was a deep, throaty roar. The coyote was already gone by this time, having bolted from the area at the first whine of the horn.

While the horn continued to roar, Acharon gathered up his pack and Murphy's handgun from the dining table. He then pulled the tank onto the porch, the horn still blaring, and pulled the door shut, making sure the lock clicked. The door wouldn't keep out a determined bear, but they were more likely to move on to easier fare.

As he walked to his truck he watched the bushes and other houses in case some predator had overcome its fear of loud noises. It hadn't happened yet, but he wondered how long it would be before all memory of humans as the feared predator disappeared from the other animals' collective consciousness. Acharon hoped that he would be long dead before then. Of course by then there would be no people left to fear or hunt.

In the truck he flicked a switch to connect the power and pressed on the accelerator pedal. The truck lurched forward and hummed as it drove away from Murphy's house.

Acharon had come to Sausalito as a child with his parents. Back then it was still a very busy place even though the death sentence of humanity was already clearly known and understood. People were about on the sidewalks and parks, talking, enjoying the summer air of that year. It hadn't been so in many places around the globe.

Religions had spasmed in shock and then anger. Everything religions had promised the masses was not coming to pass and many could not bring the two views into congruence. They lashed out at each other in some of the most violent and catastrophic religious wars ever seen or partaken in. Nuclear weapons were no longer a mysterious threat but had been used to great and terrible effect.

That had all been part of the first years of comprehension, before Acharon and Sovelet had been born. Millions of lives, now precious in their finite quantities, were lost in those early times. Eventually, however, the religions had spent themselves and cooler heads were able to propose more sensible actions for the waning decades of the human race. That was when they began to plan for the terminal future, for the Last Wave of humanity.

No one expected or wanted those left until the end to suffer from disease or hunger or even illness. On the eve of humanity, the great dawn of humanism was born. Scientists, engineers, inventors, even politicians, all came together to begin building a world that would look after those who would be the last. People like Murphy and Acharon and Sovelet.

That was why even now Acharon had access to an electric pickup truck despite none being manufactured in the last hundred years.

It was also why they could still get medical help and treatment even though there wasn't a single doctor still alive. All the knowledge of the doctors and medical schools had been programmed into the medi-pods and the larger medi-facs. Not only could they diagnose what was wrong with Sovelet, they could heal her, too. They'd yet to be in any situation that the medi-pods couldn't fix.

Which was why Murphy's death was a blow, coming how it did. Though Acharon could see how Murphy might have reached his last conclusion, he was silently worried that Sovelet would arrive at a similar one. He wasn't willing to let that happen.

02

Sovelet wasn't in front of the medi-pod center as Acharon slowly turned his truck into the parking lot for the medi-pod facility. Dozens of cars covered in guano and moss made the flat lot look like a field of burial mounds from the early centuries. Instead of mighty warriors and queens buried beneath the loam, only their chariots were entombed.

The cars had been parked and abandoned here by people who'd come down to the waterfront to take a ferry for one final ride. As local populations slid from thousands to hundreds to tens, the remainders chose to make the move to San Francisco or Oakland to live in the enclaves. They'd chosen to congregate for companionship, to not be alone as their own end came. Some of them later regretted their decision. Especially those who'd joined the San Francisco enclave.

Every town in America had, at the least, a basic medi-pod that could set bones, sew stitches, and diagnose nearly every common disease and ailment. Optimistically, the medi-pods had been programed to help with the delivery of babies. It was one program that had never been used.

Bigger towns had more sophisticated medi-pods that could go as far as treating cancer, printing out the pills needed and performing the occasionally necessary invasive operation to remove malignant tumors. In the cities there were also medi-facs, huge facilities with medi-pods that could do anything any doctor could ever dream of doing. Acharon had an eye bio-printed and attached at the San Francisco medi-fac. He could have used one of several medi-pods in the San Francisco enclave, but for safety reasons friends had moved him in an emergency pod to the bigger facility. They were, in Acharon's opinion, the greatest invention left for the Last Wavers.

Acharon turned the truck's steering wheel, weaving past the buried cars. He drove up to the front door of the building. Inside, Sovelet waved, a thin smile on her face. Each piece of what Acharon saw was part of a puzzle picture that didn't have a happy image.

He waved back and got out of the truck to hold the passenger door open for Sovelet.

"You don't want to just walk over?" she asked as she slipped onto the seat.

"Coyotes are a little frisky today," he said as he shut the door. He could see by the way she sagged into the seat that she couldn't have made the walk without several long breaks along the way.

"Was that why I heard the horn?" In the great silence left by humanity's exit, unnatural sounds traveled farther with fewer ears to hear them.

Acharon nodded. "Drove them away from Murphy's."

"Poor Murphy. They can't get in, I hope."

Acharon stepped on the accelerator and the truck gave a little lurch as it rolled forward.

"Everything's locked and the noise will work as a hindrance memory for a time. But nothing short of a very hungry and determined bear should be able to get in."

They turned west onto a long stretch of moss once called Bridgeway. The wheels spun several times until they kicked out enough moss and dirt to reach the old pavement and regain traction. At one time, in cities and towns large enough to still have a population, automated street cleaners moved along the major arteries. They washed and scrubbed away the attempts of Mother Nature to reclaim the lost land, keeping it clear for the few vehicles that still used them. Sensors in the roads not only guided the cleaners but counted traffic. When the traffic density dropped below some determined value, the machines would ignore those streets, turning their attention to the ones used most.

Bridgeway, the main artery for Sausalito, had been one of the most used streets. When it was dropped from the cleaning route Sovelet had gone into the system and changed the numbers to keep the street clear for another decade. Discounting the occasional elk herd or coyote, Acharon was the only one driving the streets anymore.

Parking lots between Bridgeway and the water had never been designated for cleaning. This was why Acharon went the long way, down Bridgeway instead of through the parking lots. Some were already on their way to becoming forests. Bridgeway was a smoother ride and all of Acharon's concern was for Sovelet's comfort.

"If he'd stayed with us we probably could have gotten him to the medi-pod on time."

"I can't disagree with that," Acharon said. He also thought that Murphy would have been less likely to off himself if he'd been in more frequent contact with them.

Acharon turned the truck back into the parking lot, slowly maneuvering over the bumpy surface. He could no longer tell curb from road. Once again he pulled up to the door of a building. For years he'd still parked in the parking lot and walked to the doors of the medi-pod center, the food depository, and even here at the diner, even though they'd been the only people in Sausalito for thirty years. It had taken Sovelet pointing out that the whole town was theirs and it was simpler to just park in front of the building; no one was likely to complain.

"Well, I'll miss his humor," Sovelet said.

Acharon could see her smiling and shaking her head as he hurried his way around to open her door. He knew she was fully capable of doing it herself but he wanted to care for her, to let her know that he was always going to look after her.

He opened the door with a flourish. "Madam."

"Yes, you have a sense of humor, too," she said as Acharon provided an assisting hand.

"I wasn't trying to be funny."

"Not intentionally." She mollified him with a peck on the cheek.

They walked arm in arm to the doors of the diner. He could feel the pull of her arm against his, an unconscious request to slow the pace. At the diner, he opened the door for her. He followed her through, shutting the door behind.

There had never been a lock on the door since the diner was first installed. Only private residences had locks after a time. Even now, Acharon and Sovelet no longer bothered to lock their doors. Like Murphy, they made sure to completely shut the door. This keep intrusive and curious animals out of their homes. As predators and scavengers were increasingly less concerned about humans it became more important to make sure doors and windows were properly closed to keep them outside.

"The usual seats?" Acharon asked. There were twenty tables set around the room. Pictures, much faded, were secured to the walls. Several brooms were propped against them, too, near the recycling hatch. There were six touchscreen terminals for ordering. Four had a large X made with tape across them. Near the terminals there were stainless steel shelves with sliding hatches at their back ends.

They sat at a table in the middle of the room. It was slightly more worn than the other tables around them. Acharon could have moved tables around but he'd become attached to the table's scratched and decade-worn surface.

"Thank you," Sovelet said as he held a seat out for her. "The usual please."

"Of course."

Acharon went to one of the two touchscreens not X-ed out. He'd been the one to cross out the other screens as they became too difficult or impossible to repair. Contact brought the screen sluggishly to life. Acharon used the time to turn and check on Sovelet, masking his intentions with a smile. A beep turned him back to the screen. He scrolled the screen, flicking past the numerous items lined through as sold out. Sovelet could have easily edited the screen information to remove unavailable food items but, again, Acharon had resisted the change. He liked seeing all the items on the menu as he made it down to the lentil mushroom loaf with mashed potatoes and creamed spinach. It wasn't necessarily their favorite meal to have, but Acharon knew the state of the inventory and wanted to save some of the other items for birthdays and anniversaries.

He pressed twice for the loaf dinner and two iced teas. The screen flickered to a different screen showing their order, which hatch to expect the meal from, and the order number that would indicate their meal was ready. The order number automatically reset at midnight so they were always number one.

"It'll be a while," he said to Sovelet. "Apparently it's their busy period."

"We have such lousy timing."

There was a brief moment of silence, slightly awkward for Acharon. He'd hoped she'd say something without prompting. When it appeared she wasn't going to offer, he finally spoke.

"So, what was the diagnosis?"

"Our meals are ready." Sovelet indicated the number blinking over the opening hatch behind Acharon.

He hurried over and brought the steaming plates on a tray to their table. The iced tea glasses sweated condensation as he set them on the table.

They started their meal in silence. Acharon's question remained unanswered for now.

"Could we get dessert?" Sovelet asked after eating less than half of the meal.

Acharon wiped at his mouth with his napkin as he pushed back his chair. "I think we can still get vanilla ice cream. Coffee?"

"That'd be nice."

Again, Acharon went to the terminal and made the order. This time he waited by the hatch to keep himself from trying to force the conversation again.

The ice cream and coffee arrived as quickly as the meals, rolling through the hatch on a second tray.

He served them both again and sat down. The ice cream was synthetic but still creamy. The coffee was actual instant coffee and not yet synthetic, though the diner was equipped to provide it if ever the need arose.

As he sipped his coffee he glanced at Sovelet who was looking at her ice cream while taking tiny bites. After several bites she stopped and laid her spoon next to the bowl. The ice cream was slowly melting into a pool of itself.

"I have lung cancer," Sovelet said. "Not surprising, I suppose, after having lived so long."

"But, the pills."

Part of the great medical surge that saw the development and deployment of the medi-pods was the development of pharmaceuticals that extended life, improved brain health, and fought off every illness except the common cold. Though they were 147 years of age, they were both fit and, as far as Acharon had believed, very healthy. But no system is ever perfect.

"No one ever said they were a hundred percent certain."

"But there are other medications for fighting cancer," Acharon said. The ice cream in his bowl had melted without him having eaten more than one bite. "The medi-pod here can print them."

Sovelet shook her head, a sad smile in accompaniment. "Too late for the pills. The medi-pod says I need full lung replacements."

"'Replacements'? It's in both lungs?"

"That's what the medi-pod said. I looked at the scans and I'm compelled to agree."

Acharon stared at Sovelet. Even with all the rapid advances in medicine and pharmacology, cancer still had the power of the boogie man. It may not have had the same power to frighten as it had in their youth, but it still could scare a person into silence.

"You going to say something?"

"We have to go to the city," he said.

"Maybe." She stirred her ice cream-stained spoon into her cold coffee, leaving thin trails of artificial cream.

"Maybe? No, definitely."

"Ach, it's been a long, good life. But we can't live forever."

"That doesn't mean we just give up," Acharon said. Murphy's note came to mind. "It's the wrong attitude."

"Why keep going? Can you tell me why we keep going? Day after day on our self-made island. The last person we knew, now dead himself."

"You said there were more people. New York? Tokyo? Cairo? Paris?"

"They aren't here, Ach." Her voice had a sad note to it that made Acharon's chest ache. "How long do we go for?"

Acharon picked up his own spoon and stabbed slowly at the thick cream in the ice cream bowl. "Until death takes us by surprise. Not because we quit, but that we were too busy to notice it had come."

"Doesn't it seem pointless?"

"When did you get so pessimistic?" He'd left the spoon in the bowl and now had a grip on the sides of the tabletop, his hands squeezing the table. "I've never heard you talk like this. I mean, I thought we were on the same page, that we were going to live our long lives together, until the end. Together."

Sovelet nodded. "Together, I know." She paused for a while. She turned to look out the large windows of the diner. After a long, slow sigh, she continued. "I imagine that it's Murphy's death. And then when we were talking on the radios I realized how few people were left. So few. And when they're gone, when we're gone...."

"That's it," Acharon finished. "I know. But that doesn't mean we have to hurry to the finish line. Besides, I'm not ready to end this. And I can't live without you. You're too much a part of me."

They had been married, by Acharon's count, for one hundred twelve years, seven months, six days. He rarely thought these days of himself, but of them as a pair, a team.

"I understand," Sovelet said after a long pause. "I wouldn't want to be alone without you either. But it's going to happen to one of us eventually."

"Then why rush it?"

They sat in a vacuum of silence that attempted to pull more pleading from Acharon. He resisted heroically, watching Sovelet, waiting. She appeared to be studying the old pictures of sailing ships on the walls. Off to the side, through the scratched plastic-coated windows, Acharon noticed the darkening sky. The day was reaching its end. They were normally safely on their island by this time.

"Okay," she finally said. "We'll go to San Francisco."

"Good." Acharon hoped his voice didn't give away the desperate fear he'd been holding back. "We'll take the Catalina over in the morning. Should be a good day for a sail."

"Sure," she said. "Why not make an adventure of it."

"Home?"

"Yes, please. I'm feeling a bit tired."

Acharon quickly cleared their dishes and put them on the reclaimer belt and pushed the button. Everything would be chewed up into a mulch that trucks used to come and remove on a weekly basis. Now, when the error light came on, about once every couple years, Acharon would go around the back of the diner and shovel it out, spreading it across the ground. Over the years, the flat ground had become a wide, broad hill.

Once everything disappeared behind the sliding panel, he hurried back to Sovelet. Now that she'd told him the problem, it seemed to him that she was more willing to rely on him for assistance. She held onto his arm, using him for support as they left the diner.

There was a whispered ding of a noise as they exited the diner. It was to inform them that their money card was being debited via the implanted RFID tag. Much like the street cleaners many things changed as the population dropped across the globe. Acharon was no longer sure when it happened, he was sure Sovelet knew, but prices had disappeared off everything. Anything that people needed or wanted was provided at no cost. This was part of the gift to the Last Wave of humans from those that had preceded them.

03

The ride back to the island in the electric runabout was a quiet one. Sovelet sat wrapped in a blanket, her face turned toward San Francisco, silhouetted by the light of the sunset. Acharon kept his attention mostly on the approach to the island. Occasionally he glanced to see if Sovelet had turned away from the city and, he hoped, was looking at him. It was something he would have found reassuring but it didn't happen.

Small solar powered lights guided him around the island to the dock that stretched the length of the island. Several other boats were tied up to the dock. The Catalina they would sail to the city waved its mast in the air as the boat rocked on lazy swells. Beyond it, a small tugboat sat squat on the water, ready to labor as needed. With practiced ease, Acharon brought the runabout up against the dock, deftly flipping the lines over the dock stanchions as the hull tapped the bumpers.

After they docked he again offered Sovelet a hand in assistance. She blinked as if coming out of a trance before taking hold of his hand. She treated him with a soft smile as she stepped onto the dock.

"I'll finish here if you want to go on in."

"Would you like a cup of tea?" she asked.

"Yes, that'd be nice."

Sovelet went up the steep and narrow stairs to the first barge. Acharon watched until she disappeared from sight.

Once he was sure she was safely topside, he turned his attention to the runabout. He disconnected the battery from the motor and connected it to the trickle charger. Over by the stairs, he pulled on a hand brake that released one of the dozen wind turbines on the island, setting it spinning in the evening breeze.

Acharon could do a lot of things. He'd built the island and their house. He'd wired everything so that it ran off solar and wind power. He'd cobbled together enough batteries that allowed him to store energy for sunless, windless days. All the things he could do, he could do because of the unique education he and most of the Last Wavers had received.

Knowing that the young children growing up would be the last echo of humanity, most nations had made the decision to give them every educational opportunity possible. This didn't happen right away. First there were the religious wars, followed by the women's revolt, the clone debacle, and conflicts related to fear and stress. It took time but eventually most people accepted the fate that humanity had made for itself.

From the first years in elementary school, he and Sovelet and other children in the Last Wave of births were educated differently than those who'd preceded them. The class sizes were smaller, usually no more than ten students. They were taught the basics but then they were given further education in science, technology, math, and engineering.

It was believed that the ability to build a machine or reprogram a computer and other technological necessities might be more useful than an education in world history. Though, they were given many classes in history as well, many of those classes focused on the last decades.

All of the Last Wavers learned about the genetically modified rice that had resulted in the end of humankind. Dust from the chaff of the rice had risen on the winds and, over a decade, covered the globe. Those that breathed it were infected. The infection tainted their sperm and eggs, resulting in every child born from that point on being sterile.

No one had known it was happening at first. It wasn't until primates in laboratories and zoos suddenly stopped producing offspring that a clue was given. All Hominoidea had been infected and that included Homo Sapiens Sapiens.

The cause was longer to determine. But when it was known, many of the executives of the company responsible were killed by angry mobs in dozens of countries. Even executives who had nothing to do with the GMO division suffered at the hands of a scared and angry population.

This history education was intended to explain to the Last Wavers why they were the last and what they could expect. And what they could expect was to be childless and most likely alone at the end of their lives.

Acharon knew all this and knew that his actions were purely selfish. He truly didn't want a life without Sovelet. He also couldn't bring himself to end his own life intentionally. Nor would he, if it were him who was stricken with a deadly disease, allow his life to sputter to a stop without first trying everything possible to remain with Sovelet. He carried no belief that there was something after death. Neither of them would be waiting on the other side.

The death of the last human would mean the total extinction of humanity from the universe. He imagined it would be him or Sovelet and he wasn't sure who he wanted to be in that position. Maybe they'd get lucky and die in their sleep, holding hands. But not yet.

With those heavy thoughts burdening his shoulders, Acharon climbed up from the dock to the first barge. The barges were of standard size, being twenty feet longer than their forty-five-foot width, common at one time in the San Francisco Bay. The first barge was the garden barge. Corn stalks were to the north, off to his right, with tomatoes in front of them, followed by lettuces and beans, and then to the root vegetables. There was never enough to make it a full year, even if they canned what they didn't eat before the vegetables began to rot. But it did provide a refreshing change from the packaged meals.

In the early days, even when the population of the world only numbered in the low millions, automated farms provided fresh produce for most of the year. Large self-guided trucks would carry produce into the towns and cities. They'd enter special buildings that held the trucks like vegetable stalls. After several days the trucks would leave. The leftover food would become compost back at the farms, and new trucks would take their place in the vegetable stalls. Theoretically the trucks should still be running. They were designed to last at least two centuries. But machines break down, roads erode, accidents happen. The last time Acharon had picked fresh vegetables from the depository was more than ten years ago. Fortunately they had already begun their own garden years before.

He took a few minutes to pick several large, ripe tomatoes. He would fry them as part of breakfast in the morning with reconstituted tofu scramble and toasted canned bread. He then crossed the arched bridge to the barge with the workshops on it. This was where he tore down, repaired, and built the electronics he needed to keep their lives as comfortable as he could. The island might lack some of the amenities of the enclave in the city, but it was emotionally better beyond compare.

The second bridge brought him to their home barge. He'd put together a prefab home he'd found at one of the Last Wave depots and brought it here. There was a small great room, a bathroom and two bedrooms. The second bedroom was Sovelet's computer room where she fixed and maintained programs and services through the Internet. She also maintained a discussion board where Last Wavers left messages, asked questions, and carried on decade-long conversations.

Sovelet's computers were the biggest draw on the electrical system. She ran several stations at a time along with a server that kept the whole house warm in the winter months. Fortunately, Acharon had installed a dozen wind turbines. Monochromatic solar panels covered the roof of the house and the work sheds. They had plenty of power. Enough for Sovelet's computers and the more mundane draws of everyday life, which was as Acharon had planned.

As he stepped through the gate of the yard fence, something he had added merely for the charm, Sovelet was coming out of the house with a tray in her hands. She moved slower than Acharon thought was right. He hurried over to her.

"Let me take that for you."

Sovelet twisted away. "I've got it, thank you. Go sit."

Acharon held up his hands in concession and went over to sit in the yard chair that was his normal spot. Sovelet followed and placed the tray on the table between the two chairs. She poured tea from a glass teapot into two cups and lifted one by its saucer for Acharon.

"Thank you," he said.

"Think nothing of it."

Sovelet sat in her chair and lifted her cup and saucer to her lap, her hands cupping the saucer while the steam, lit by strings of fairy lights hanging from the pergola overhead, writhed upward from the surface of the tea.

They sat in the quiet. The sun was down near the horizon, hidden beyond the hills behind them and the black mound that was San Francisco in the dark. Their patio faced east. Angel Island could be seen peeking around the headland that held the ghost town of Tiburon.

As the sunset became a whisper of itself, the perimeter lights on the barges began to blink on. Acharon had edged the barges with a four-foot-high railing and then attached lights to them so that no one could accidentally fall over. They were on all night, just in case. Those lights, the ones on the foot bridges, the ones around the eaves of the buildings, and on the pergola beams gave the barges a festive flair. Quite the contrast to the atmosphere between him and Sovelet.

"Nice night," he offered.

"Uh huh."

It was not the response he'd been hoping for. What he wanted was for Sovelet to feel good about their decision and to give that feeling a voice. Instead she sat in a self-imposed silence, quietly sipping her tea.

"I thought we'd go over early," he said. He talked more for himself than for Sovelet but hoped it might stimulate her to respond. "Not sure how things are working in the city. If they work at all. What's it been? Twelve years? Since we last went over?"

"Fourteen years."

"That's right." Acharon had gone to the medi-fac outside the San Francisco enclave for a knee replacement. It had been an easy ride from the marina by monorail carriage to and from the medi-fac. He doubted they would have been welcomed back inside the enclave and he wasn't sure who was left, as none of them had responded to Sovelet's inquiries over the Internet. "Think anyone's still there?"

"I've asked around. Someone, Morgan, I think, used to correspond with the Chicago enclave. She stopped four or five years back, just after the Chicago people transferred over to New York."

Acharon nodded. They were conversing.

"I guess there's only one way to find out."

"You want to stop by and knock?" Sovelet asked. "Really?"

Acharon laughed. "No. But we could wander close by and see if anyone lobs something at me."

Part of the schism in the enclave revolved around a militant attitude that some of the original members took when survivors from the Oakland enclave came across to join the San Francisco group. Oakland had put all its eggs in one basket. Medi-fac was right there next to the community. So when the earthquake came and broke things up and subsequent fires devoured the place, there was nothing left standing. The people in Oakland could have stayed, but they would have had to travel to San Francisco or Sacramento for medical assistance and food. Some of them went to Los Angeles and were never heard from. Most of them came to San Francisco. It had not been an easy merger.

Sovelet rose from her chair. She picked up the tray in her free hand.

"Where're you going?"

"To bed. Long day tomorrow."

"All right," Acharon said. "I'll be right there."

"Take your time."

It was not the usual response. Sovelet usually encouraged him to hurry along. She still had some lingering resentment. Hopefully things would be better tomorrow.

Normally he was the one reluctant to go into the city, for any reason. If the Oakland enclave had still been standing, he'd have suggested that, instead. Hell, he'd have gone there for the work on his knee even though he'd never gone close to the San Francisco enclave for the surgery. Just the thought of being there made his eye ache and his stomach roll with mental discomfort.

04

The next morning, just as the gray morning sky was beginning to blue, Acharon was swallowing the last piece of toast and gulping down the last of his instant coffee. With a peck on Sovelet's cheek he was out the door and back on the dock. Sovelet was still somewhere topside, supposedly preparing a lunch to take along. Acharon knew that more than likely she was in her office, repairing some device somewhere via the Internet or making her latest update on the blog she insisted on maintaining.

One of the last big projects, when there were still several billion people left on Earth, was the net of satellites that dotted high earth orbit like seeds on a strawberry. Built to last, most of them would probably still be in the sky centuries after Acharon and Sovelet had died.

While he waited, Acharon uncovered the sails on the sailboat. It was modeled on the classic Cal 24, sturdy and reliable. He'd managed to talk the professors at Berkeley into printing it on the SL 3-D printer before it was decommissioned along with the rest of the university. It had spent most of its hundred years sealed in a container on Pier 23. There'd been other boats to sail. This boat was to be his backup if all other available boats wore out over the years. When they'd left the enclave permanently, they'd used it to sail off into the sunset to Sausalito. It was the only ship to sail on the bay for the last twenty-four years.

With the sails uncovered, he prepped the lines for casting off. He checked the batteries for a full charge. If need be, he could swap out tired batteries for fresh ones in the charging shed. Once the main and jib were up, the solar panels built into the sails would top off the batteries used to drive the motor and other electricals.

He was making one last check of the systems, fighting the urge to go looking for Sovelet, when he heard her voice.

"Ach."

He hurried toward the stairs. "Yes, dear?"

"The basket?"

The basket being referenced was a plastic wicker picnic basket Sovelet had found in the old Last Wave warehouse in Berkeley. Along with major essentials like a basic medi-pod, clothes, foods, and shelters, it also boasted a very random collection of odds and ends. When they'd first studied the Berkeley inventory list online they'd looked at each other and shrugged. They shouldn't have been surprised. Berkeley.

"Got it," Acharon said. He hurried up the stairs and grabbed the basket by its handles and backed down the stairs. He waited at the bottom as Sovelet descended cautiously. It was a behavior he'd never seen from her until recently. Previously she'd bounded down the stairs with an enthusiasm that had been part of the reason he'd fallen in love with her.

Once down she'd uttered a quick thank you and took the basket. She was in the cockpit, securing the basket, before he could rush ahead to help her board. He resisted the urge to make a self-effacing jest and busied himself with the lines on the dock. Once she was settled in, he stepped aboard and started the engine.

A few minutes after flicking loose the last line and with the aid of a flood tide, they were free of the dock and motoring away from Sausalito and out of Richardson Bay. It was still flood tide as they left the bay with a strong wind blowing in from the ocean.

Once past the overgrowth that had been Gabrielson Park, Acharon cut the engine. The only sounds now were the lapping of water against the hull and a chorus of gulls flying overhead.

"Do you need any help?" Sovelet asked as Acharon began cranking the winch that would take in the line that unfurled the main sail.

"If you want to take over." He stepped back and presented the winch to her. He was worried that she might take the challenge.

She smiled sweetly. "I'm good."

"Your loss." He smiled, relieved that she remained sitting. With the sails up and the wind coming over the starboard rail, Acharon pointed the bow of the boat toward the Presidio. He knew that with the incoming tide they would be moving sideways as much as they were moving forward. If he did nothing else, the boat would be looking at Pier 39 or further by the time they reached the city. He hoped to be tied up at a dock before the ebb tide. If they didn't, their day would get longer as he fought the six knots of tide attempting to pull them out of the bay.

Acharon found some humor in the fact that he'd been sailing for over a century. Who could ever have hoped to make that claim back in the days when sailing ships ruled the seas. Men barely made it into their forties and now here he was, in his hundred and forties. Three lifetimes from those early days, two lifetimes from just several generations past. And now, as they sailed to the city to replace Sovelet's damaged lungs, he felt that one lifetime of any length wasn't enough time to spend with her.

A windblown shout caught his attention and pulled it back into the moment. He looked back to see Sovelet grinning and pointing off the port side. He twisted around to see what had caught her attention.

A pod of dolphins had come up beside them. About thirty of them had caught up with the boat and were pacing it, their backs arching as their snouts emerged and then disappeared below the water's surface. It was an enthralling sight, even if it wasn't the first time he'd seen a pod of dolphins in the bay. Decades back, when the number of cargo ships entering the bay in a month could be counted on one hand and fishing boats stayed tied to docks collecting nothing more than barnacles and seagull guano, the first pod had entered the bay.

Those dolphins had been a harbinger of things to come and over the years whales had been seen, followed by killer whales. The number of sea otters had exploded along with that of sea lions. It was as if the vacuum of humanity was being filled by every wild species that had long been driven from the area.

There were days, when Acharon needed to be away from the enclave in the city, that he would sail out into the bay and just heave to and watch the wildlife flex, spread its wing and cover the bay. It had been said in the enclave that if you couldn't find Acharon anywhere in the city, look out to the bay. Forty years ago he'd suddenly become the only ship on the bay. Next to time spent with Sovelet, sailing was his second great pleasure.

They stayed west of Alcatraz as they approached Aquatic Park. Sometimes he liked to sail around the old prison, just to see it up close and examine the decay, but today he didn't want to waste the time tacking back toward the Marina District.

Acharon began the process of rolling in the main sail and then the jib. He switched to the electric motor just outside the crumbling breaker wall for the park. A few sea lions, sunning themselves on the rocks, watched with sleepy eyes as the boat motored past.

Decades ago this had been the best destination to dock their boat when coming to the city. The automated trolley line still ran back then and was just a couple of blocks away. But the piers were now too rotted for safety here, and like many other float docks they'd been destroyed by the population boom of the sea lions. The automated trolley line's cable had snapped the same year they'd abandoned the city, so Acharon knew that wasn't going to be available.

Their final destination was the UCSF medical advancement center near the east end of the Golden Gate Park. There'd once been a dental college there but it had been transformed to suit the needs of the Last Wave. Being situated on a hill, the building could be powered by wind turbines when energy from power plants was no longer viable. When the enclave was established at Huntington Park, a modest medi-fac was built in the old offices of the Grace Cathedral.

They'd put one of the big medi-pods at the back of the old offices, where a boys' school had been. Like the ones at the medi-fac it could do any major medical procedure. It could print any internal organ, short of the brain, and then surgically replace it into a human body. It was a truth he knew from experience.

Most medicines could be printed at any medi-pod. For the really complicated compounds, again a trip to the center or the enclave's major medi-pod was required.

But before they could concern themselves with medi-facs and

printed organs, they had to find a place to dock their boat. There were several places that they'd used before, but like much else of the city, it was worn out and overgrown.

It was clear as they motored slowly into the park that there'd be no docking here. The Maritime museum dock was mere pilings jutting up willy-nilly from the water. Several boats from the docks on the other side had broken free from rotted lines and banged about the marina until they clogged the entrance and then slowly sank for good measure.

"Moving on," Acharon said. He turned the boat around to leave the park and paused, his hand reducing throttle.

"What?" Sovelet asked.

Acharon pointed with his chin. Just above the wall that embraced the beach, a wolf sat, looking in their direction.

"I thought they followed the elk," Sovelet said.

When the last citizens of San Francisco had contracted, for the most part, into the enclave, wildlife began to make free use of the Golden Gate Bridge. Acharon had watched deer meander across when he still lived in the city. From Sausalito he'd seen elk cross, heading south. They'd made a majestic sight, backlit by a setting sun diffused by fog slowly rolling in. That same night he'd heard the wolves howling up by the old remains of Vista Point.

The animals had moved back and forth across the bridge over the years until the center span had finally collapsed.

"Maybe the elk never left." Acharon gave the wolf one last look before twisting the throttle, exiting the park waters and turning south.

They continued to motor along the waterfront. From here they could see that the flora had gotten a good hold of the city. Ivy climbed up the sides of buildings and weeds and bushes grew from every possible crack and cranny. From their observation point off the shore, the city looked as if it was blanketed in greenery, the buildings themselves seeming to have grown from the ground just like the plants that surrounded them.

The view was deceptive. Acharon knew this. He knew that once they stepped ashore they would find many streets overgrown, but major arteries would be mostly clear. There were also the monorails with their individual carriages that they could board outside the old

Ferry Building. It would take them directly to the medi-fac by Golden Gate Park. In no time they would have Sovelet in the surgical medi-pod and just as quickly she'd have new lungs and they'd get back to their life on their island, away from San Francisco.

They motored past pier 39 and its breaker wall with the boat slips behind. There'd been plenty of slips still useful last time they were here and the walk to the Ferry Building wasn't far.

"Doesn't look good," Sovelet said. She had gone forward, holding onto the mast for balance.

"Nothing?"

"Not that I can see. Do you want to go in and look?"

Entering past the breaker wall could put them at risk of snagging on collapsed docks or old boats that had torn loose and sank, barricading the lanes. If they grounded their boat on anything they would have a difficult time getting not only ashore, but back to their home.

"Better not chance it," Acharon said. "We'll just work with twenty-three."

Twenty-three was a pier farther south, past the Ferry Building. It had been converted into long-term storage for Last Wavers. The pilings had been replaced when the new building had been built and stocked with many useful items. That was assuming no one from the enclave had sabotaged it.

They continued along the waterfront at a pace unlikely to challenge a tortoise. Flood tide had ended and ebb tide was just beginning. Acharon wanted to be tied up before the strong outgoing current made it nearly impossible to maneuver the way he'd planned to do at pier twenty-three.

Sovelet stayed forward by the mast, her eyes scanning the city. Acharon watched the shoreline, careful of other sunken ships or large floating debris.

Several times something ashore moved and caught his eye. Once it was a single wild pig trotting in the opposite direction as if it had a date to keep. The second time it was several deer grazing on bushes and grasses growing along the edges of the Embarcadero. They lifted their heads and watched the boat passing and then slowly returned to their grazing on the undergrowth.

Even despite having watched the changes slowly occur, watching the city go from a thriving hive of human activity to a ghost town, it still surprised Acharon. Buildings succumbing to nature's relentless touch. The appearance of creatures one would once have had to travel far up into the hills of the Santa Cruz mountains or farther afield to see. Now all of that which had been kept at bay by civilization's progress had retaken what had once been theirs.

"Twenty-three." Sovelet was pointing to the long building that jutted out onto the bay. Even though it was newer than any of the other buildings along the waterfront, it looked equally as worn. A hundred years had that kind of effect.

"All right," Acharon said. "We'll try for the waterside ladder." He'd practiced a similar approach several times at home, off their island. But there the water was more protected. Here, things were a lot more active.

On the narrow back end of the building an even narrower ladder reached down from an equally narrow walkway that surrounded the water sides of the building. The ladder plunged into the water, its end invisible in the dark water of the bay.

Fortunately for Acharon he'd had plenty of time over many years to come up with solutions of unlikely scenarios. This was one he'd solved several times, improving it each step of the way. He was ready for the challenge.

They couldn't just dock the boat against the pier pilings. The constant rough motion of the bay waters would dash the boat against the pilings repeatedly until the boat was finally broken. They could drop an anchor and anchor out, away from the pilings, but then they'd have to swim to the ladder, which was nearly as dangerous as docking the boat against it. Then there was Acharon's way.

"Prep the anchor, dear," Acharon called out.

Sovelet gave him a thumbs-up and moved to the bow, one hand holding firmly to the lifeline. At the bow, she unstrapped the anchor. She held tightly to the lifeline and the anchor rode and turned to watch Acharon. Acharon had turned the boat and moved it about thirty feet, pointing the bow away from the pier.

"Now."

Sovelet released the anchor rode and the anchor splashed into the water. The anchor rode spun out behind, following the anchor into the deep, dark water. Acharon had three hundred feet of thick line attached to the anchor chain. He had plenty to work with.

Once the anchor settled on the bottom, Sovelet secured the line to a forward winch. Acharon reversed the engine setting the anchor, digging its flukes into the mud.

He kept the engine running, pulling against the anchor just enough to keep the boat in place as he ran other lines in a preplanned configuration. As Sovelet stepped back into the cockpit, he handed three lines to her, each marked with a colored ribbon.

"I'm going to back the boat to the ladder. Take these up with you. Tie the blue one off at the top of the ladder, the red to the right stanchion, the green to the left. Pull them until they're pretty straight."

Sovelet repeated the instructions and Acharon clapped her on the shoulder. "You got it."

He returned to the wheel and brought the engine speed up. At the same time he pushed down on a button that reversed the winch that held the anchor line, slowly feeding out more line as the boat backed to the pier.

When the boat was inches from the ladder, Sovelet stepped across. She held the ropes in one hand and climbed up with the other. Acharon watched with misgivings as she released a rung and quickly grasped the one above. He started to suggest a different strategy when Sovelet's feet slipped off the rung she'd stepped on.

"Sovelet!" His panicked yell matched her scream. She'd reflexively released the lines she'd been carrying and reached for the rung where her other hand gripped it. Just as quickly she reached back down, pulling one leg up. She pinched the lines between body and thigh. Her actions slowed the escaping lines until she could once again grab all three.

"Hang on, I'm coming," Acharon said. He'd have to risk losing the boat, but it was nothing compared to Sovelet's safety. As he reached the stern, she looked back at him, her face fixed with a hard look.

"No."

Her single word stopped Acharon from leaving the cockpit. He knew the tone and wasn't foolish enough to challenge it. She was going to fix the problem and woe to anyone who got in her way.

"Sovelet?" His body shook with tension.

"Just wait." She'd managed to get one leg hooked over a rung after she'd rescued the lines. She used that leverage to get her other foot on another rung. She stopped then to slowly open the hand that had kept her from falling into the bay.

Most everything that the Last Wavers would ever need had been designed to last. Metals had polycarbonate coatings designed to last centuries. But mother nature was persistent and with the help of continuous sea water baths had worn away the plastic from the ladder. Wherever the plastic had been worn away, there was now a thick layer of rust.

Sovelet's hand dripped blood as she flexed it.

"How bad?" Acharon asked.

"I'll live," Sovelet answered. She raised her hand and grabbed the next higher rung. She winced as she pulled, putting pressure on her abraded palm and fingers. "But I'm going to need a doctor."

"I know one," Acharon replied, relieved to hear her good humor.

Nevertheless, he remained by the stern of the boat until she was standing firmly on the walkway. Once there, she gave him a thumbs up, blood still seeping from her closed fist and began tying off the ropes as Acharon had directed.

When she was done, Acharon tossed his pack up to Sovelet, aiming for her feet so she wouldn't have to use her hands. It was a ten-foot toss on a boat bobbing on the swells and the pack teetered on the walkway edge as it landed. Sovelet hooked it with her foot and pulled it to safety. The picnic basket was an easier toss and landed near where Sovelet had pushed the pack with her feet.

Acharon showed a relieved smile before he killed the engine and then hurried forward to the bow. He made some adjustments at the winch with a second line before lifting a duffel bag and a coil of rope that he hung over his shoulder. He then hurried back to the stern, trailing the line that was coiled over his shoulder, and quickly ascended the ladder.

Acharon dropped the line and duffel bag. He took Sovelet's hand, still shiny with fresh blood, and examined it while asking, "Are you okay? I mean besides this?"

She shrugged. "Shoulder hurts. Ribs on the same side feel tender."

"Can you hang on a few more minutes and we'll take care of all that?"

"I don't have any other plans."

"Good." He gave a quick kiss on the cheek and got back to work.

The line he'd carried was the other end of the one with the blue ribbon Sovelet had brought up the ladder. He set the coils of line down on the walkway and took up the end Sovelet had carried. Bracing himself against the top of the ladder he began to slowly pull on the line. The line went down to the boat, through several pulleys and then to the forward winch. As he pulled the line it turned the winch which took up anchor rode and pulled the boat away from the pier. Sovelet moved back and forth between the other two lines, using one hand to let out slack as they began to pull against the boat's progress.

Acharon stopped when the boat was twice its length from the pier. He stood and brushed his hands together. Job well done. He smiled at Sovelet. "Welcome to San Francisco."

"Dangerous place," Sovelet said. She held up her bloody hand for emphasis.

05

"Let's get you taken care of." Acharon slipped his backpack onto his shoulders and grabbed the duffel bag. "This way."

Sovelet hooked the picnic basket with her good arm and followed. Her closed fist left a widely spaced, crimson dotted trail behind them.

With Acharon in the lead they walked around the outside of the pier twenty-three building. They had to move slowly along the narrow walk until they reached the street. Acharon pulled a pair of bolt cutters from the duffel bag to cut through the lock holding the chain link gate shut. They stepped out onto the Embarcadero, yet still inside a chain link perimeter. The fence embraced the half of the sidewalk in front and several meters beyond the width of the building. The fence had three points of access, two gates for people to walk through and one large rolling gate through which trucks and other vehicles could pass.

"The entrance is over here." Acharon led the way to a glass door, its exterior coated with dirt, moss, and the random guano bomb from a passing pigeon or seagull. The handle took a few shakes and yanks, but it finally conceded victory to Acharon, who pulled the door open and waved Sovelet through. They were in a small entry with a second glass door that lacked the debris of time and opened without hesitation.

In the near dark, Acharon felt along the wall until he found a metal box. Inside the box was a single large switch that he lifted from down position to up. A weak glow filled the ceiling as tens of thousands of LEDs slowly woke and began to emit light.

The inside of the warehouse was a sterile white with a light coating of dust. The air was stale with a hint of freshness wafting in from the open door they'd entered the warehouse through. The freshness evaporated as the glass door clicked shut. The bands of LEDs across the ceiling now filled the cavernous building with a cheery white light.

Across the floor, lined and stacked, were crates of various sizes and cargo containers of differing lengths. Almost all of them were painted white. Near the front of the building was a prefab office. Next to that was a forklift. A power line snaked its way from the forklift's battery compartment to a charger on the wall.

Acharon began scanning the rows of containers. "It should be near the front."

"Maybe there isn't one here."

"Nonsense, there's one in every warehouse." His face brightened. "And there it is."

He hurried over several rows where a bright red container squatted between two equally large white ones. It should have been at the front of a row, preferably close to the entrance. But as it was near the roll-up door, it was about half correct in its position.

Unlike the hundreds of other containers with their double-door ends, this container had a regular door and windows. Acharon pulled the door open. He stepped back as quickly, wrinkling his nose as a high concentration of hospital antiseptic smell rolled out of the doorway. Sovelet, close behind, stepped back, waving her blood-washed hand in front of her face.

"New car smell?"

"New hospital smell." He reached in and flicked the switch his hand came into contact with. Lights snapped on as if a half century or more had never passed. "In we go."

It was like stepping into a different world. Outside was the cold and hard world of a long-term warehouse. Inside the container was a medical office with waiting room chairs and even a couple of hundred-year-old magazines and a screen that could probably play canned game shows. Most important were the medi-pods, one at each end.

Unlike everything else in containers in the warehouse, the med-clinic had specialized deep cycle batteries and a direct connection to the building's electrical. Even without the building's power supply, the med-clinic still had enough power after seventy-plus years to deal with a dozen minor injuries before they needed to be recharged.

Sovelet set the picnic basket by the door and used her good hand to tap the screen, slowly bringing the system to life. She entered data that reconnected the medi-pod's system to the internet, finding and retrieving her medical records. A few more bits of data and the pod's door slowly but effortlessly slid open. "I'll be right back."

Acharon stood just outside the door to the medi-pod as it slid shut. It was rare for him to be standing on this side. Sovelet had a luck that Acharon seemed to lack. In similar situations, where he might find himself with a gash in need of sealing, Sovelet would have walked away with barely a scratch. So, seeing her in a medi-pod for more than a check-up wrung his heart and made his stomach ache.

Inside the medi-pod, Sovelet waved and lay back. The privacy curtain slid out of the end wall of the pod and surrounded Sovelet. In more advanced models the walls would have just faded from clear to opaque.

Acharon sighed and turned away. There wasn't any use standing and staring at a curtain that would reveal nothing to him. He paced the waiting area for several minutes and then walked out the door to stare at the ceiling overhead. He didn't want to be here.

He used to love the city. He loved the energy it emitted even in the waning days of humanity when the population was in the tens of thousands. They'd still held the parades and street parties. They'd still had the same contentious arguments in city hall. Especially when it came to the location of the city's enclave. Many people wanted the enclave in Golden Gate Park. He'd liked that idea, too. He'd helped design that enclave. There'd been quite a blow up when the location was revealed. Huntington Park hadn't even been in the top five choices.

"Ach? You okay?"

Acharon spun around. He smiled at the sight of Sovelet, her hand shiny now with a synthetic skin coating that would slowly wear off as her hand healed. He loved seeing her after not seeing her for a while, even if that while was mere minutes.

"Yep. You ready?" He went back into the med-clinic and returned with the pack on and the duffel bag and picnic basket in his hands.

"You really think the carriages are still working?" asked Sovelet. She took the basket from him as they started walking back toward the glass-door entrance. From there it was a short walk to the Ferry Building.

When the governments of the world began preparing for the Last Wavers' time alone, they designed equipment and supplies to last a lifetime. Unfortunately for the Last Wavers, many of them had lived or continued to live much longer than that expected lifetime. Even Acharon and Sovelet had already exceeded the life expectancy that the world had planned for. This was evident in the failed automated farms' produce delivery and the collapsed Golden Gate Bridge. However, many things, like the automated diner and the medi-pods had easily exceeded expectations.

"I don't see any reason why not," Acharon said as he held the door open for Sovelet to step past. "There are maintenance carriages that should keep the rails clean and intact. The worse thing that could happen is that there aren't any transport carriages at the Ferry Building station. And I doubt that's going to be the case."

At the gate in the chain link fence, Acharon paused and looked around. The wolf they'd seen near the aquatic park was a long way off. But wolves could travel fast. Always best to be cautious. Once he was satisfied the wolf wasn't lurking about, he pushed against the gate. It resisted his initial effort. It took several back and forth motions to scrape away dirt and other debris before it swung wide enough to allow them to pass. Just like he would have back home, he shut the gate before continuing.

As they walked to the Ferry Building, he eased back on his pace, hoping that Sovelet wouldn't notice him taking it easy. Fortunately the walk was short and she seemed to be too focused on breathing to notice what he'd done.

"There you go." Acharon pointed to the elevated monorail lines. The station jutted up from the middle of the Embarcadero, reaching up and out to embrace the monorail tracks. "Our chariot awaits."

This was only one of the monorail's termini. From here the monorail went south, turning on Market and north to the Marina District. Either direction would work. All they had to do was board and within a half-hour they should be disembarking at the medi-fac center.

"If it's working," said Sovelet as they mounted the steps to the load platform that would take them south.

"Of course it's working."

Acharon followed behind, allowing Sovelet to set the pace. She moved with less spring than he could recall in all their years together. He knew it wasn't just the battering from the ladder. She paused at each of the two landings to look around before continuing.

The platform, like the rest of the city, was slowly being overtaken by nature. Moss grew in the shady areas and long grasses pushed up through dirt-filled cracks. Eventually larger plants would push the cracks farther apart until the platform shattered and collapsed under the stress. A thousand years from now there would probably be no clue that the monorail platform ever existed.

Once on the platform, Acharon moved ahead of Sovelet to reach the first carriage in a line of ten. He'd been confident about the carriages working when talking to Sovelet, but he harbored a deeper concern that they might actually be defunct.

While Sovelet wiped a spot on a bench clear enough to sit, Acharon touched the outer access pad of the carriage. He had to brush away a thick layer of dark dust to even see the panel. The markings had faded from long exposure to sunlight and weather but he knew where to push.

Nothing happened.

"Not working. Hang on."

Acharon moved around the carriage, stepping gingerly across the rail to access panels meant for the initiated. He managed to pry one open and squatted for a better look. The electronics inside were caked with mouse hairs and droppings and the skull of one unfortunate mouse. He pulled a knife from his belt and prodded at the panels, removing most of the animal refuse but revealing that the mice had tried to make a meal of the wires and plastic.

"Definitely not working," he said. He stepped back onto the platform. "If the next one works, we could probably pop the brake on this one and push it ahead of us."

"All right," Sovelet said. Her voice lacked optimism from Acharon's point of view.

Unfortunately the second and third carriage also refused to acknowledge Acharon's insistent prodding of the access panel.

"Nothing?" Sovelet asked. She seated herself on a bench, picnic basket resting on her thighs.

Acharon prodded the wiring of the third carriage a few more times despite the knowledge that it wasn't going anywhere.

"Not here," he said. "Maybe we'll have better luck on the northbound track instead."

The monorail had been used sparingly during the last years Acharon and Sovelet had spent at the enclave. They'd probably been used even less once the two of them had departed for their Sausalito hideaway. The leftovers of humankind were failing as should be expected. Acharon would just prefer they not do so when he needed them.

Sovelet had already risen and started back to the stairs. It was a torturously slow trip for Acharon, down one set of stairs and up another. He resisted mightily the desire to ask her if she was feeling okay, did she want to take a break, could he help? It may have taken him a few decades to work it out, but he'd learned early on not to try and coddle her.

As soon as Sovelet's feet touched the top stair of the northbound platform, Acharon slipped past her and jogged to the front carriage. He could hear a long and heavy sigh escape from Sovelet as she wiped a spot on a bench and took a seat.

Again, it was the same process with the same results. Three carriages at the front of the line, each degraded to the point of being inoperable. Acharon felt frustration rising in him like bile after eating something noxious. This was supposed to be easy. Bring Sovelet to the city, deliver her to the medi-fac, get new lungs, go home, and continue enjoying their lives.

"Ach."

He turned to face her, swapping a pained look for a grin. "I guess the maintenance crew dropped the ball on this one."

He'd been the maintenance crew for the last years they'd spent in the city.

"What about that one?" She pointed to the last carriage, on the south end of the line.

"The carriages are all wired and geared to go one way. These go counterclockwise. The ones on the other platform go clockwise."

She smiled at him in the way that warned him he was missing something. It also told him she was enjoying that fact. "But aren't you one of the engineers that helped design this whole thing?"

There it was. He knew these damn carriages inside out. He was supposed to. It'd been over half a century. Still, he wasn't senile, so why not?

He held up a finger in pause. "Hold that thought."

From his backpack he dug out several multi-tools and went back to the south-end carriage. With a little sweat and several muttered curses he was able to remove two of the outer panels that allowed him to access the workings of the carriage. He began to fiddle with connections. The more he traced and tugged at the wires and connectors, the more he remembered.

He jumped to his feet. "Got it!"

"It's working?" Sovelet stood, the basket held in two hands.

"What? No. Not that kind of got it. I meant I know what to do now."

Sovelet sat back down while Acharon managed to bring the carriage online and get its doors to slide open. Inside, the carriage was nearly as fresh as the last day someone rode inside it. There were a few cobwebs but that was the extent of it. Two seats were along each of the end walls. Under the one on the south side, Acharon found what he was looking for. The carriages were all built to the same specs. It was just several connections in the controls that affected the direction. This enabled a passenger to just engage the carriage and it would go in the intended direction without being told which direction that was. Disabling that would require the passenger to indicate the direction of travel.

He found and quickly removed the connector. With the seat back into place he wiped the dust of decades off his hands and stepped into the doorway.

"And finally, there we are," he said. "Just like I told you. Comfy ride to the medi-fac. Ladies first."

He handed Sovelet across the threshold. As she took a seat at the front, Acharon flipped open the interior control panel. His touch woke the waiting computer. It took longer than he recalled from past journeys for the computer to finally show the destination screen. Things were older. He reasoned that he probably moved more slowly than he remembered.

The screen showed the route of the monorail through the city. A blinking green dot showed the current position. Acharon touched a gray dot near the medi-fac by Golden Gate Park. A new window on the screen popped open and requested a forward direction. The gray dot turned yellow once he chose clockwise on the new window. The doors to the carriage slid shut.

"We're on our way," Acharon said. He sat on the seat opposite Sovelet.

"I'm really surprised you got it working."

"Because I helped design them?"

Sovelet laughed. "No. Of course not. Because they're old. What? A hundred years?"

They both leaned into the momentum as the pod jiggled forward, picking up speed.

"The system is a hundred and twenty. These carriages are only fifty."

"Honestly?"

Acharon shrugged. "They were put on the rail fifty years ago. They may have been built long before, but they were kept in hermetic storage. So they should have been as good as brand new at the time they were unsealed."

Sovelet gave an accepting smile and turned to look forward, watching the city begin to slide by. She had to watch through a dirt and guano streaked windshield. The edges of the window were trimmed in moss and short grass. It gave the carriage an organic feel to go along with the musty interior smell. Acharon would have liked to have had a day to clean the interior. Maybe when Sovelet was in the medi-pod he'd slip down and scour it clean.

"Ach!"

"What?" Acharon rose to his feet, reaching for Sovelet.

"Stop the carriage. Stop the carriage!"

Without questioning, Acharon reached for the emergency stop on the computer panel. But just as he was reaching, the emergency stop signal covered the entire screen and the carriage slowed and then jerked to a stop.

"What happened?"

Sovelet stood and pointed past the grimy windshield. "That."

A hundred feet beyond them, the monorail track was gone. Building facade lay in a rubble ruin with the missing monorail track poking out from underneath.

Acharon looked up to the left and then the right. To the right, part of a building's face was gone, revealing ragged floor ends that remained as the wall fell away.

"From an earthquake?"

"It's been a few years," Acharon said. "But we did have, what was it? A six or seven?"

"Six point two. But that shouldn't be enough to tear the face off a building."

Acharon started touching buttons on the screen. The carriage began moving backwards. "The face of a two-hundred-plus-years old building? It could. Not every building got sprayed."

"Can't go the other way?"

"I don't have any way to remove the carriages that aren't working. If there were a repair carriage available we could use it to lift the bad ones away. But if we had a repair carriage we could just take it to the medi-fac."

"So we can't get to the medi-fac," Sovelet said. Her tone was matter-of-fact.

"We can walk," Acharon said. He braced himself as the carriage lurched back in the direction from which they'd begun.

"You're kidding."

"I hope," Acharon said. He lapsed into silence as he began thinking of the warehouse on pier 23. Redundancy had been the watchword back in the planning days for the Last Wavers. So it was very likely that the things he hoped were in the warehouse were there. But there was always the chance that they weren't. There were other warehouses, but none were near the shoreline. He didn't like the idea of having to move through the city on foot; Sovelet's lungs probably wouldn't be able to keep up.

Acharon's reverie was shaken by the carriage thudding to a stop. The doors sighed open and they stepped onto the platform once again.

"This looks familiar," he said. His reward for his humor was rolled eyes, courtesy of Sovelet.

"And now what do we do?"

"I could go and check the north-end carriage on the other track. We didn't think of that idea until we were on this side."

"Our idea?" Sovelet asked. The look on her face told Acharon she already knew the answer. "You can check, but I'll wait at the bottom of the stairs.

"Fair deal."

Over on the other side, Acharon rooted around in the north end carriage, hoping to make something click. Despite the answer he was getting, he gave it several more minutes to change its mind before returning to the base of the platform where Sovelet rested on the bottom stair.

"And?"

"And now back to the warehouse."

"And then?"

"And then I'll build us a car."

06

"You want to help?" Acharon asked. They'd made it back to the warehouse easily enough. He felt she looked more tired than she should and hoped she wouldn't take his suggestion seriously.

"You know I wouldn't know what to do. Do you think that office has computers and access to the Internet?"

Acharon waved an arm to indicate the whole of the warehouse. "It should. If not, there's probably plenty out there."

"I'll check the office." Sovelet turned and walked her slow, tired walk to the prefab office, her steps echoing as she climbed up the thin metal stairs.

"And I'll see if the forklift has any life in it," Acharon said. He spoke to himself as Sovelet was already at the door to the office.

While some parts of the world that the Last Wavers would live in could be automated, like the farms and the monorail carriages, it was realized that much of the items being produced could not be made in the low population future. This was the beginning of the warehouses.

Across the United States and most other countries that were taking the future of the Last Wavers seriously, warehouses were constructed with the idea that they would stand for decades and hold items that anyone remaining might need or want so they could be accessed. This was different from the food depositories that held tons of sealed cans and dehydrated packets of food stuffs. Here there was clothing, shoes, tents, hammers, nails, decks of cards. Nearly everything that a person might need to survive in the world alone.

Everything was preserved, sealed hermetically to minimize the decay of time. Clothes were sealed in airtight packets that had been flushed with nitrogen. Computers, rifles, hammers, anything that couldn't be preserved in a soft packet was set in an aluminum container, flushed with nitrogen, and then sealed like soup, waiting for someone to pull the tab and access the contents. Then there were the cargo containers, sealed with silicon at every joint and crease, desiccant dumped by the wheelbarrow loads across the floors, and then finally sprayed over with a plastic sealant similar to what had been done with many buildings around the world. Some of the cargo containers merely held repetitions of what was in crates and barrels plainly visible on the warehouse floor. But others held the very thing that Acharon sought. That is, if they filled the warehouse properly.

In the rush to prepare the world for the Last Wavers, not all things went as planned. Food items had been mislabeled, computer programs had been launched riddled with bugs, and plans were not always thought through to their conclusion. So while there should be several varieties of automobiles somewhere in the warehouse, there was always the slight odds that someone screwed up and another warehouse was missing hammers and nails but had twice as many cars.

"Container 'A four one.'"

Acharon stepped out of the cab of the forklift. It had been hooked to a trickle charger connected to solar panels on the roof. The forklift had a full load on three of the batteries, the fourth was damaged and probably slowly corroding the others.

"What?"

Sovelet disappeared back into the office. Before Acharon could even wonder if he'd done something wrong, she came back and held up her two-way radio. Acharon quickly dug his out of his pack.

"I'm sorry," he said into the radio. "I didn't hear what you said."

"It's hard to yell. Not enough air. Anyway. Try container 'A four one.'"

"Car?"

"I found the manifest files on the computer. It just says 'transportation.' I hope that doesn't mean motorcycle."

Acharon smiled and waved. "I'm sure it's not. Thank you."

"You're welcome." She disappeared back into the office.

Acharon sat in the forklift and turned the key. Indicator lights began to glow bright. The forklift gave the impression it was ready to work. Acharon pulled on the lever to raise the front of the forks and the machine responded with a sudden pulse of action. The forks clanged as they bounced upwards.

He smiled sheepishly even though no one had seen his first effort. It had been, by his quick reckoning, nearly forty years since he last drove a forklift. That was when he'd put the house on the barge.

With the handle for drive shifted to forward he slowly stepped on the pedal. At best guess, the forklift had remained in one place for at least sixty years. Long enough for solid rubber tires to develop a flat spot. The tires groaned as they were forced to roll from the flat spot at their bottoms and make new contact with the smooth concrete floor. Each rotation of the wheels was emphasized by a thump as they fell onto the flattened sections of rubber.

The forklift moved forward as directed by Acharon and he steered the machine down the center aisle. Behind him, tire crumbs marked his progress.

There were two rows of short columns. They were parallel to the front wall and continued all the way to the back wall, fifty-five columns in each row, odd numbers to the left, evens to the right. Down each column, on the fronts of containers or on the ground in painted squares of the same size, were labels A, B, C, up to K. Bigger warehouses had columns that required double letters as the slots for containers went past twenty-six in the column.

The transportation container was in column forty-one, on the left. The container, being labeled with an A, was the first container in the column. Its location made Acharon's job easier.

He guided the forks under the container and slowly pulled on the lever to raise them. Once it was off the ground, he tilted the container back several degrees. The container rocked, making Acharon nervous as he pulled the lever into reverse and stepped on the throttle pedal. The slow, steady beeping of the back-up warning accompanied him as he maneuvered the container to the front of the warehouse. He set it down near the charging station.

He caught a glimpse of Sovelet in the office. She looked up. He waved and she replied with a hand-blown kiss.

Acharon hopped down from the cab of the forklift and went to the container. He pulled up on the levers that kept the doors locked and shut. The doors didn't open, but he knew that with the plastic sealant they wouldn't. The expectation was to score the plastic with a knife several times to break the seal. There was an easier way for those in a hurry.

From under the seat of the forklift he pulled out two long lengths of chain with hooks on all four ends. He hooked the chains to the fronts of the container doors and then wrapped them around the backs of the forks, using the hooks to hold the chains in place. He then jumped into the cab and reversed the forklift, causing it to pull on the chains, which pulled on the doors.

In the first moments the plastic held and the entire container slid forward several feet. Then, with a sucking, popping noise, the doors flew open, rattling the chains like angry ghosts. The event was finalized by the container doors clanging against the container's sides and the collective sounds echoing through the warehouse.

Acharon turned off the forklift and climbed down to have a look in the container. At the front were steel drums with the words "tires" and "batteries" stenciled across them. Beyond them he caught the reflection of a windshield. He stepped closer to look at the vehicle that was going to take them to the medi-fac. He nodded appreciatively as he took in the view of the four-wheel drive, hard-top Jeep, complete with a bank of lights across the roof and roll bars inside. Behind the Jeep, in the gloom, he could see at least two more.

Now all he had to do was get one running.

With the help of the forklift he pulled out the pallets of canned tires and batteries and then dragged out the pallet with the jeep strapped to it. The jeep rested on wood blocks, waiting for wheels and tires to be added.

Acharon spent the next two hours getting the jeep put together. He stopped once, when Sovelet called him on the radio to come and have lunch. They sat on the metal stairs outside the prefab office rather than eat within its close-walled confines. Sovelet asked a couple of questions about the progress with the Jeep. Mostly they ate in silence. Acharon ate quickly, eager to get back to work.

He still had to mount tires, grease and lubricate bearings and joints, and install the batteries for the electric engine. Once the batteries were completely charged he figured he should be able to get several hundred miles before they needed recharging. Plenty of energy to get to the medi-fac and back.

Charging the batteries, however, quickly went from a minor task to a large problem.

Acharon had pushed the Jeep over to the charge station. The forklift had been attached to a trickle charge that kept the batteries full. There was also a quick charger available. Acharon hooked the Jeep to the charger but got only a weak trickle of energy. At the rate it was charging, the Jeep wouldn't be ready to operate for the next thirty-six hours. He checked the wires and connections, troubleshooting everything that he could think of until he was left with one final possibility.

He went to the office to find Sovelet. No expense had been wasted on the office. It was a typical, faux-wood-paneled room with several desks, chairs, a couch. All the comforts of home without the warmth.

"I have to go topside," he said as he stepped into the office.

Sovelet was tapping rapidly on a keyboard, stopping to talk after a few more bursts of typing. She spun the chair to face him.

"The roof?"

"Yeah. I'm not getting a good charge on the Jeep's batteries. I've tried everything and all I can think of is that the solar panels are blocked. You want to come with me?"

"Is there an elevator?" Sovelet leaned over to look out the window as if she might see her answer.

"No, it's one ladder, straight up to an access hatch."

"You should have suggested elevators when they began these things."

Acharon smiled. "They didn't actually ask for my input. I was busy elsewhere. So you're going to wait here?"

"Here or outside."

"Outside?" Acharon turned to look toward the entrance to the warehouse. He couldn't see the outside from there but he recalled the weeds and grass and bushes. They'd seen the one wild pig and the deer

53

as they'd gotten closer to the warehouse. Could there be something more threatening? Like the wolf? "Are you sure?"

"Yes." She laughed. "I'm just going to go and stand outside. The air in here is heavy. It's tough to breathe. I'll stay inside the fence."

"Will you take the shotgun?"

Sovelet sighed. "All right, I'll take the shotgun. But I'd probably have more success with the air horn."

As no one had a clear idea of what the world would be like in the final decades of humanity, everyone had been trained in the use of handguns, rifles, and other forms of explosive self-defense. They all spent a couple of weeks between school years on the range. They learned to fire them and maintain them. Acharon had taken naturally to the broad armory of weapons made available. Sovelet had been reluctant to use them, doing just enough to pass competency tests.

"Take both? Just in case."

"Fine," Sovelet said. She stood and started toward the door. "But don't be long, then."

Acharon followed and outfitted Sovelet with the shotgun, loaded with salt rock and plastic pellets, and a quart container air horn.

"You have your radio, too?" Acharon asked.

"Yes, but I'm running out of hands."

They worked together to clip the air can to her belt at the back and the radio was hung from a lanyard around her neck.

"Reminds me of when we were kids," Sovelet said. "They used to over-protect us. Pads on every joint just to ride a bicycle. Safety glasses to play volleyball and basketball."

"You're right, they were overprotective," said Acharon. "I'm not. These days aren't like those days. You know it's true."

"I do." She checked the shotgun, ensuring that a round was chambered. "Be safe."

"You be safe. And don't go far."

Sovelet gave him a kiss on the cheek and walked toward the entrance. Acharon followed her until she reached the glass door. Once the door drifted shut, he searched for some brooms and long-handled scrapers. As a hopeful afterthought he unpacked a water hose and brought it along, too. Before the climb he slipped on a pair of thick microsuede gloves. Only then did he grab the first rungs of the ladder.

The access to the roof was forty feet up the ladder. Fortunately, it was wrapped in a safety cage. If he slipped, he wouldn't fall far; but it would still hurt. He tied the handles of the brooms and scrapers together and tied the rope to his waist. He shouldered the water hose and started to climb.

He was doing something that, in the past, a man half his age would have had a difficult time doing. He knew that the end of humanity was a double-edged sword for himself and the rest of the Last Wavers who were still alive. There'd been many rapid advances and reluctant revelations of drugs and surgical techniques that improved the life of everyone alive but especially the Last Wavers.

Having taken the supplements, the inoculations, and the mystery treatments from adolescence onward, they'd been blessed with extra-long and extra-healthy lives. Though it was likely that Murphy would have disagreed about it all being a blessing. There were probably others that felt the same way. However, if it weren't for all the benefits fostered on him and the others, Acharon would not have arrived at the top of the ladder, ever.

Though the handle to the access hatch had been unused since the building was first made, the sealed air and advanced lubricants on the joints allowed Acharon to easily release and push it open.

There was a burst of sharp noises, like high-pitched clapping as hundreds of startled birds quickly took flight.

Acharon climbed through the hatch to stand on the slightly angled and very dirty roof of the warehouse.

He took a moment to take in the view. Out past the Embarcadero, a forest was stuffed in between towering buildings that once held thousands of people who had lived and worked and walked in them and around them. Cars, trolleys, people, all had filled the Embarcadero itself. People had once traveled from around the world to walk here and sightsee here. Even when the world's population had finally dipped below one billion, people came to San Francisco. It was certainly less crowded. Lines to get into tourist sights were practically nonexistent.

Turning, he looked through the tall trees until he caught sight of the obelisk. Every major city in the United States had one just like it. Many cities across the world had one, too. This one had caused quite a ruckus when it was installed. The obelisks were set on solid ground and visible to potential alien visitors or a new species rising to prominence. In San Francisco it was right where Coit Tower used to stand. They knocked it down and put the obelisk up. People were mad about that. Probably because no one ever asked them. The governments had gotten sort of narrow-visioned around that time.

The obelisks were humanity's "we were here," scratched across the surface of the globe. Four of them floated in space at all of Earth's Lagrangian points, stable positions between Earth and Sol. On every one of them was etched the story of Homo Sapiens Sapiens, as told by each country's centric view.

They all told the story differently but they all ended at the same point. It wasn't when humanity sterilized itself. It was when the last scientist admitted defeat in the efforts to clone a human. Right before that was listed the failure to suspend life through cryogenics. Only then did humanity admit defeat. Only then did they put all their energy into preparing the world for the Last Wavers.

That's when they began to improve the medi-pods, the monorails, and the high-efficiency solar panels. But even the best solar panels were no match for seagull guano.

Eighty percent of the roof was covered with solar panels. If they were cleaned to a pristine condition, they could charge several dozen Jeeps at once and in just a few hours. In their current condition, Acharon was surprised the forklift had any power at all. But that was just a testament to the quality of the cells on the roof.

Off to the right, Acharon spotted the water spigot. He slowly made his way to the spigot, being careful not to slip on the guano, dirt, and feathers that coated everything. He grabbed the handle of the spigot and tried to turn it. Debris, and possibly corrosion, jammed the handle. He continued to worry at it, twisting one way and then the next. Finally the handle turned. Then it came off the spigot, still in his hand.

"So we're doing this the hard way," he said and dumped the water hose on the roof.

He started with the scrapers, loosening the debris on the first ten panels. After the debris was loosened he went back over with one broom to sweep away as much as would come away before coming back with a brush to rub off any more that he could persuade to come away. When he'd finished with the first ten he moved on to the second ten.

The hours were going by too fast. Acharon did not like being in the city any longer than he had to. He felt safer and more at home on their island.

"Ach?"

Acharon put down the second broom and keyed the mic on his radio.

"Sovelet? Are you okay?"

"I'm fine. How much longer are you going to be up there?"

"Depends. Where are you?"

"I'm inside," Sovelet said.

"Can you go look at the rapid charger for the Jeep and see what the panels are putting out?"

"Okay. Give me a second."

Acharon pocketed his radio and returned to sweeping with the second broom on the last panel of the second ten. It would probably take him all day to clean every panel off.

"Ach?"

He grabbed his radio. "I'm here."

"It's indicating two hours to a full charge."

Two hours? He wouldn't mind waiting that long. He could use something to drink. Too bad the water line was a bust.

"Okay, I'll be right down."

He left the brooms and scrapers where he dropped them and ignored the useless water hose. At the bottom of the ladder he looked around for Sovelet.

"Sovie?"

"Here." Sovelet was standing by the entrance to the warehouse, looking at the door's glass window or through it, Acharon wasn't sure.

"Going back outside?"

"No. Come here."

Acharon trotted over to the door. "Something wrong."

"I don't know," Sovelet said. "It's just weird."

"What's weird?"

Sovelet pointed to a stand of narrow-trunked pine trees. "Can you see him?"

Acharon was bothered by the word 'him.' Was there still someone alive in the city? And who was it? It would be rotten luck if it were someone he'd left the city to avoid. But as he studied the trees he quickly ascertained that 'he' was not a human.

"The dog?"

"Yes."

The dog in question was larger than any dog that Acharon had ever seen. It was bigger than any coyote he'd encountered. It looked as big, if not bigger, than the wolf they'd seen that morning.

Many people had illegally let their pets loose rather than subject them to the euthanasia program. They reasoned that their pets deserved a chance to live a life. Acharon understood, but he'd been witness to a few domesticated dogs and plenty of cats falling prey to the more aggressive and more wily feral dogs that quickly began to dominate the city when the population fell under a hundred thousand people. They'd had a hundred years of Darwinian breeding.

"What about him?"

"He's been there since I first stepped outside."

"Are you sure?"

"It's my lungs that are having problems," Sovelet said. Her voice had a tinge of fear and anger. "My brain and my eyes are fine."

"Sorry," Acharon said. "Give me the shotgun."

Sovelet handed him the shotgun and stood back as he walked out the door.

Acharon stepped outside. The dog remained in among the trees. He had to agree with Sovelet, the dog did seem to be watching in their direction. Acharon scanned the area to make sure that there weren't other dogs off to the sides, lying in wait. He'd once gotten himself hunted by a hungry pack of coyotes when they'd had a rare snow winter. He'd killed most of them and lied about it to Sovelet. It had been too scary a situation to repeat.

Once assured that there weren't any surprises nearby, he walked slowly toward the fence. The dog gave every appearance of focusing on Acharon, watching him as he reached the fence and swung the gate open. He checked again for other dogs and then continued, crossing the Alameda. When he was less than thirty feet away the dog turned and disappeared into bushes beyond the trees. Acharon caught a glimpse of it looking back over its shoulder just once before it disappeared completely.

Acharon took a few minutes to look around and make sure that there wasn't anything else to raise concern.

"Maybe he was just lonely," he said as he entered the warehouse. "Missed human companionship."

"That dog wasn't old enough to have ever been around humans."

"Well, it's gone now," Acharon said. He rested the shotgun against the wall by the door. "You going to go back outside?"

"No." She followed him back to the charge station.

Acharon checked the connections and examined the readouts. An hour and a half and they'd be ready to roll. Plenty of time to locate some nice canned water.

07

Acharon pulled on the chain that raised the second roll-up door. The controls and gears were designed so that one roll-up door had to be closed before the chain on the second door would move. This worked like a canal lock, controlling access to and from the warehouse.

When there was enough space to drive under, Acharon stopped pulling on the chain and waved to Sovelet, sitting in the driver's seat.

He could hear the click of the lever shifting from park to drive, followed by the whisper whine of the electric engine as it drove the gears that turned the tires, moving the Jeep forward. Once Sovelet had moved the Jeep past the door, he released the chain and stepped to the other side. A second chain was accessible outside and he used it to lower the gate.

The whole process had taken ten minutes. Acharon fought the urge to check the sky. He was pretty sure it was well past noon, close to two or three in the afternoon. It being late summer, they still had plenty of daylight left. Probably not enough to get back home. Maybe they could get back here. The couch in the office didn't look that uncomfortable but they'd be in the best position to sail back to Sausalito with the morning ebb tide.

Outside the building there was only the chain link fence to get past. It was held shut with a simple latch and opened with a little effort once dirt and grass was pushed out of the wheel channel with a knife tip. Acharon shoved the gate open. Again he waved Sovelet past and, out of habit, rolled the gate shut. Someone in Sausalito had once left the door to the clinic ajar and it took weeks to get the skunk smell out of the waiting room. The rule was simple: shut the door, you don't know what'll wander in.

With the gate latch properly set, he returned to the Jeep where Sovelet was shifting over to the passenger seat.

"You know which way you're going to go?" she asked as Acharon buckled himself in.

"I'm going to keep it simple. We'll go up Market, to Van Ness, to Oak, then around the park. We'll adjust as necessary, but that should do it."

"You don't want to go the other way?"

Acharon shook his head.

"Don't like those hills?" He could see the impish smile pulling at her lips.

He stepped on the accelerator and turned on the left signal blinker as the Jeep rolled forward. He laughed at himself and turned off the blinker as he turned on to the Embarcadero. "I guess there's no need for that."

"I guess not." Sovelet smiled and then turned to look at the wild foliage that was taking over the city.

They drove several blocks in silence, each looking at the changed city. Nature was already being allowed to encroach when they'd Acharon and Sovelet first moved to the city. It was an acceptance of the simple fact that Mother Nature was taking back land stolen from her by human will. It was also a realization that there weren't enough people in the city to keep her at bay any longer. So they had pulled back from the edges and Mother Nature had pushed in behind them.

Now her green tendrils reached far into the bones of every town and city. Ivy grew as high as it could on skyscrapers and blanketed the smaller buildings. Ledges collected dirt, which harbored grass and wildflowers, which prepared the thin ground for future bushes and trees. Eventually she would tear down what humanity had so willfully erected in its own honor. It would all be reduced to grassy hillocks and mounds that no future generation would uncover in wonder.

Yet, for now, there was some humanity left in the city, even if the count was only two.

"Did you find out anything?" Acharon asked. "On the computers in the office?"

"It took a while to find access to the Internet." She turned to face him as she spoke even though he had to give most of his attention to the green and bumpy road. "I looked for any signal that someone was still living here. I didn't find anything. And the bulletin boards don't show any action from this region except for my signature."

"So no one's left."

"No one that has access to the Internet," Sovelet said. She turned back to look out the side window as they neared the corner of Embarcadero and Market.

Her comment left open the option that there could be someone still here. Someone who wanted to stay off what grid there was left. And if that were the case, then there might still be life up at the enclave. There was only one person paranoid enough to cut access to the outside world. Acharon was okay with their paths never crossing again.

"Do you think we should stop there? Just as a courtesy?"

"I'd rather not ever go there again," Acharon said. "My eye twitches just thinking about it."

"No it doesn't."

Acharon maneuvered the Jeep around a rusting hulk of a car that had burned at some time in the past. Moss covered the hood and weeds pulled at the rear bumper.

"All right," he said. "It doesn't twitch, but it doesn't mean I'm eager to go back."

"I understand. Oh! Stop the car!"

Without hesitation, Acharon moved his foot from the accelerator to the brake and brought the Jeep to a quick stop. The tires slid on the thin layer of dirt and weeds of the roadway. They slid several feet, spinning a few degrees clockwise.

"What? What is it?"

"Look." Sovelet was pointing to a patch of grass that looked unchanged from the days of lawn maintenance.

"Deer? You stopped me for deer?"

"Not just deer," Sovelet said. She stabbed her finger against the window. "Does. And fawns. They're so cute."

While the world was filled with self-pity and occasionally self-contempt over the end of humankind, no one really considered the female babies being born that would be denied the natural opportunity to bear their own children. For those born in the last ripple of the Last Wave of humanity, they never saw living human babies, never bore them, never cared for them. And while they'd been born sterile, that did not mean they weren't born with the natural desire to reproduce and nurture their own offspring.

Sovelet had a desire to nurture that was as strong as any woman's. She'd taken that passion out on kittens, fostering them whenever she found them. This had become more difficult with each passing decade. Cats were the second biggest loser behind primates. They were easy targets for bigger predators, especially cats that had the wild bred out of them. Those that survived adopted nocturnal habits. Acharon had spent many a dark night prowling the streets of San Francisco with an open can of tuna, a bottle of reconstituted milk, and an animal trap. When their last cat had died about ten years ago, which was a vague number that Acharon knew Sovelet could properly pinpoint, he'd hunted for weeks until Sovelet had asked him to stop. She'd managed to pacify her biological instincts, spending days clicking through gigabytes of baby photos she'd scoured off the Internet and saved on a separate hard drive.

Acharon shifted the Jeep into park and set the handbrake. He sat in silence with Sovelet while she watched the does and fawns pulling at the short grass, her hand pressed against the window. Acharon imagined her trying to feel the maternal energy of the does. He knew they were wasting time, but he wouldn't rob her of the little things she treasured.

Sovelet stayed statue-still, her breath making a blur of fog across the bottom of the window. She was like that for several minutes before she gasped in surprise.

The does, with the fawns at their heels, suddenly bolted south along the edge of the Embarcadero. They quickly disappeared in some distant bushes.

"What happened?"

"I'm not sure," Sovelet said. "They just bolted. Oh, wait. That's why."

Acharon had to look around Sovelet to see what she was pointing toward.

Three large dogs came trotting out of the trees, north of where the deer had been. Their tongues lolled over the edges of their mouths. They came into the clearing where the deer had been grazing and sniffed around before sitting. Their attention wasn't on the frightened deer. They seemed to be focused on the Jeep.

"Does that one look familiar?" Sovelet asked.

Acharon studied the three dogs. There'd been wild dogs in Sausalito, but none of them compared in size and stature to these.

"Could be," he said. "Why? You think he ran off to get several of his buddies to come and attack our car?"

"You can't tell me they don't seem interested in our presence."

"I wouldn't say that." He switched the car from park to drive and stepped on the accelerator. The car gave a little jolt and then began a steady roll forward, in the same direction as the deer. "They're probably curious. Who are we? What are we? There's a very good chance they've never seen a human before."

"They might have a memory of humans. A shared memory or something. Some animals feared humans though they'd never been threatened by them. That's because previous generations had learned that people were dangerous. Somehow, that got passed on."

Acharon watched the dogs through the rearview mirror. "So they have some deep, uncontrollable desire to play fetch?"

"Laugh, go ahead." Sovelet was twisted in her seat, looking back where they'd come from. "But those dogs were very interested. Still interested."

"I see them," Acharon said. With the rearview mirror he could see them trotting along, fifty yards behind the Jeep. Not too close to be surprised by anything Acharon could do, but close enough to stay in visual contact. "Seatbelt."

Sovelet spun back around and fumbled for her seatbelt. When Acharon heard it click he pressed further down on the accelerator. The engine whined as it spun faster and the car picked up speed. The rough surface of the roadway jolted them. Sovelet grabbed the handhold above the door for extra stability.

The dogs fell back but then went from trotting to a long-legged lope that brought them back to their original distance.

"Okay," Acharon said. He pressed down further on the accelerator and the car surged forward.

"Ach," Sovelet said. He could hear the stress in her voice.

"It'll be okay," he said. He was looking for the park that separated Embarcadero from Market Street. When he saw it he turned the Jeep as sharp as seemed safe, leaning against the turn and easing off the accelerator until they were facing Market. The Jeep fishtailed. He adjusted the position of the front wheels and when the Jeep straightened out he pushed down on the accelerator again. The Jeep bumped and bounced forward at an aggressive speed. The dogs disappeared behind the turn, separated from the Jeep by the trees and bushes.

When the Jeep reached the comparative smoothness of Market Street, Acharon applied more pressure with his foot. He fought a momentary battle with the steering wheel as it attempted to spin out of control.

"Ahead!"

"I know."

Ahead was the collapsed building facade and the monorail track. The debris completely blocked the width of Market. As the Jeep approached the blockage, Acharon yanked on the steering wheel and the Jeep turned a hard left onto Spear Street.

Acharon kept the speed up until they reached Mission. He slowed, braking to a right turn onto Mission.

"Anything?"

Sovelet twisted in the seat, wrestling the shoulder strap out of her way. She studied the road and the corner at Spear while the Jeep continued down Mission. "I don't see anything."

She slumped back into her seat. "They were really following us. Why were they following us?"

They continued down Mission, the speed of the Jeep reduced to minimize the bumping and jolting.

"Like I said. They were probably just curious. Maybe they were dangerously curious. I certainly don't think I would have gotten out to toss a ball with them. They'll find something else to distract them."

"Normally I don't get creeped out by animals," said Sovelet. Acharon knew she meant what she said. Her love for all things fauna was a primary reason they'd adopted a vegetarian diet. "But the way those dogs came out of the trees and just stared at us, it made the hairs on my neck stand up."

"Well, don't worry. They're probably off attacking helpless fawns."

"Acharon."

He grinned mischievously and then turned his attention to the road. Despite the slow decline of humanity that allowed those left to keep their world tidy, cars and trucks were still abandoned when they ran out of battery energy or fuel. People would just get out and find another vehicle that had a little juice left in it and drive it until they reached their destination or needed another vehicle.

People in the Last Wave got sloppy as the numbers continued to shrink, despite all the planning efforts.

Acharon guided the Jeep around several cars covered with dust that had collected long enough to become dirt and go to seed. The buildings along Mission had the solemn silence of a natural canyon. There'd been a time when the sides of the buildings would echo with sound of the city, creating a background din that was ignored until it was gone. Now there was only the whine of the Jeep, the chirp and chatter of countless birds in the trees, and early afternoon shadows that hung off the west side facades, draped across the road.

They drove in their own silence until they reached Van Ness and took the hard hook to the right. Van Ness stretched out before them. The trees that made up the median were thick and tall, the branches hanging low to the dirt and weed covered road.

The turn onto Oak didn't improve the situation. The trees had grown unchecked for decades and the roof of the Jeep was smacked repeatedly by the low branches. There was no way to avoid them and Acharon found himself foolishly apologizing every time they smacked against the roof.

"Ach."

"I know," he said and then grimaced. "I'm trying not to apologize. It just happens."

"Not that," Sovelet said. She rapped the window with one knuckle. "That. They're back."

Acharon eased off the accelerator and looked across Sovelet. "Where? Got it. I see him. Does he look familiar?"

"I don't know. No, actually, it doesn't." She turned her head, tracking the dog that had appeared on the right corner of Laguna a half-block ahead and was now nearly alongside them. "It's not the first one I saw. He was solid brown. Cinnamon brown. This could be one of the others that had a white splash across half its face. I'm not a hundred percent sure."

Acharon pressed on the brake, bringing the Jeep to a stop. As soon as the Jeep came to a stop the dog turned and trotted down an alley. Its route was partially hidden by bushes and weeds. Acharon had the impression that the dog had turned to its left which would send it toward Golden Gate Park, the same direction they were heading.

"Well, it's gone now."

"Just a random dog?" asked Sovelet.

Acharon shrugged and pressed on the pedal again. "Dogs are pack animals. If it's in the city, and surviving, I'd think that it must belong to a pack."

"But not the same pack."

"I can't answer that," Acharon said. "We're a long ways from the waterfront. I don't know how much territory they'd need here to survive. And crossing into another pack's territory wouldn't be allowed. That dog we just saw could just be curious like the others."

"Curious enough to chase us?"

Acharon thought about the direction the dog had gone. "I doubt it."

They lapsed back into silence as they continued up Oak Street. Sovelet was leaning forward, hand on the dash, her eyes scanning the streets and doorways as they drove past. As the Jeep jolted to the side, she looked at Acharon who was quickly correcting the path of the Jeep.

"Sorry," he said. His focus should be on the road, not looking for spectres like Sovelet.

Sovelet had returned to scanning the side of Oak street and

Acharon returned to shifting his gaze from the road to Sovelet and back to the road. The dogs were certainly unnerving, with the way they seemed to be watching and following. But he chalked that up to natural curiosity. They and the Jeep were a new element in the city and the dogs, in all likelihood, were investigating to see if Acharon and Sovelet were some kind of threat.

But it was Sovelet's deep concern that bothered Acharon. He didn't know if her reactions concerning the dogs could have any effect on her breathing which would affect her lungs. A lack of oxygen could affect her reasoning processes. A poor response to the wrong situation, like the dogs, could become life threatening. He just needed to get her to the medi-fac. Once there, the machines would diagnose, fix and repair, and have Sovelet as good as new. Then they could get back to their island and forget all about San Francisco and the dogs.

"There! Right there!"

Acharon lifted his right foot. The Jeep slowed as he scanned the area where Sovelet was pointing. They'd passed over Masonic Avenue and were approaching Ashbury. Acharon caught just a glimpse of several dogs loping along amongst trees and bushes of the panhandle of Golden Gate Park. He couldn't get a very good look as they were constantly disappearing and reappearing among trees and bushes. He was certain it was more than one, definitely more than three. His gut, with a twist of anxiety, told him it was a pack, a hunting pack.

"I see them." He put his foot back down on the accelerator and they were pushed back into their seats as the Jeep leapt forward.

"They're after us, aren't they?"

"I don't know," Acharon said. "Maybe. But we're in a car. They can't get us."

They were speeding down the rough and bumpy surface of Oak. Several times Acharon felt his backside catch air, leaving the seat. The pull of the seatbelt kept his head from hitting the roof with each bounce.

They passed by Schrader and were a block away from the main body of Golden Gate Park when the pack swarmed out of the panhandle and onto the roadway.

"Ach, there's a lot. A dozen. Maybe more."

Acharon took a quick peek in the mirror to see the pack sprinting behind the speeding Jeep. They were massed together, the afternoon shadows masking their individual actions. They looked like one very large hairy blob to him.

"Hang on!"

He pulled down hard on the Jeep's steering wheel and the vehicle ground its way around a corner onto Stanyan. The rear of the Jeep fishtailed and the tires spun uselessly for several seconds before the wheels bit into the roadway. The Jeep's motions had Acharon regretting his aggressive driving. The sudden traction shoved the Jeep forward once again and they lurched ahead of the dogs that stumbled their way around the corner.

Acharon pushed the accelerator against the floorboard, his leg muscles flexing with the effort, willing the Jeep to go faster. He knew he was right, the dogs could not get them inside the Jeep. But if the Jeep were somehow disabled, they would be trapped inside and he doubted the dogs would suddenly become bored and leave all at once.

From the size of the pack it was possible they would just wait Acharon and Sovelet out. He wasn't going to let that happen. He had to get them to the medi-fac. Then he had to get them inside.

As they sped past Beulah Street, Sovelet shouted. "Some of them, they've left."

"What?"

Acharon was wrestling with the Jeep's steering wheel, keeping it on all four wheels as they barreled down Stanyan. He was focused on getting to Parnassus. Maybe some steep hills would tire the dogs out.

"About half," Sovelet said. "Half of them just ran off."

Acharon's stomach twisted again. He'd seen too many wildlife videos. "Which way?"

"Through the park. Why?"

Acharon didn't answer. Sovelet quickly worked it out.

"You think they're going to head us off? They'd have to know where we're going. How can they know that?"

"I don't know," Acharon said. He turned the wheel to the right. Sovelet bumped against him but they were on Parnassus now. Up the hill and they'd be at the medi-fac.

Parnassus Avenue from Stanyan was a long slope upward. Not as steep as some of the streets over in Pacific Heights, but Acharon hoped it was enough to wear the dogs out. They'd been running for blocks and some of them, if his gut was right, had been following them since they'd left pier 23.

"Still with us?"

"I'm not sure." Sovelet was quiet while she watched the corner. "They're coming."

Acharon's leg ached from pressing the accelerator hard against the floorboard. He leaned forward instinctively, urging the Jeep to go as fast as it could. He looked at the speedometer and groaned. They needle was falling. It was falling slowly but it was still falling.

"I think we're leaving them."

"Really?" Acharon couldn't believe it. He chanced a quick look over his shoulder to verify Sovelet's statement. They had indeed put some distance between themselves and the remaining dogs. "Wow."

He looked forward just in time to see a small pack of dogs charging up from Willard Street.

"Hang on," he shouted.

Out of the corner of his eye he saw Sovelet hug the seat back, wrapping her arms around it and pressing her head against it. Her eyes were closed shut.

Acharon always did what he could to please Sovelet. She didn't want him killing animals so he'd switched to practices that drove them away or convinced them to be elsewhere. But they'd never been hunted by a pack of anything. There'd been the one time, a decade ago, with the coyotes. That had been the scariest situation he'd ever been in, up to that time. It hadn't been as scary as this and the coyotes had never tried it again. These dogs were aggressive enough that he was sure that Sovelet's moratorium might not extend to here.

Nevertheless, Acharon pressed a thumb against the horn symbol on the steering wheel with as much pressure as his foot was below. The horn startled and scattered several of the dogs. The rest bounded to the sides as the Jeep reached them.

Several loud yelps as the Jeep barreled past implied that not all the dogs had gotten completely out of the way.

The noises caught Sovelet's attention.

"What just happened?"

"Sorry," Acharon said. In the rear view mirror he could see that all of the dogs were still standing. Several were favoring a foot and one looked like its hind quarter was slick with blood.

"You hit them?"

"I'm sorry, Sovie, it couldn't be helped."

Several of the dogs had restarted their pursuit of the Jeep.

"In this instance, I'll give you a pass." She twisted back around, sitting down and grabbing for the support grip over the door. "They wouldn't have been as gentle."

They were a block away from the medi-fac. Acharon could see the turn into the courtyard ahead to the left.

"No I don't think they would have. Or will be."

Sovelet looked over her shoulder. "Still? This is like some nightmare."

Acharon agreed but he didn't have time to voice it. He turned the Jeep sharply and shot through the narrow entrance to the courtyard. Ahead there was a garage-like entrance where the automated emergency vehicles would have backed in to unload injured patients.

There was no time to turn the Jeep around. Acharon slammed on the brakes as the Jeep approached the entrance and it slid into the garage. He didn't bother with shifting the Jeep into park. Instead he flung his door open, throwing off the seatbelt. He paused long enough to grab the shotgun that had been bouncing around behind the front seats and ran for the button that controlled the roll-up gate. It was a gamble but he was sure it would work. He hoped that it would still work.

As he approached the opening he saw the first two dogs racing through the entrance to the courtyard. He pointed the shotgun in their general direction and pulled the trigger, ratcheted a second round and pulled the trigger again.

The exploding sound of the rounds echoed sharply in the courtyard. Again, a sound and possibly a little salt rock caught their attention. The dogs skidded to a halt and ran back through the courtyard entrance, tails tucked.

Acharon reached the button and slammed an open palm against it. He could hear the mechanisms whining in surprise, being asked to perform a task after decades. But everything had been built to withstand the decades and slowly the gate complied.

The gate lowered slowly. Too slow for Acharon. He ratcheted the shotgun as the largest dog he'd ever seen came loping around the outer wall of the courtyard and stopped halfway between the entrance and the gate where Acharon stood with the shotgun at the ready. He tried hard not to believe it was the same dog from the waterfront.

The dog was tan and short haired. Physically, it looked like a cross between a Rottweiler and a Rhodesian Ridgeback. But its eyes were not like any dogs Acharon had ever seen. The dog was studying Acharon and the medi-fac entrance with a tilt of the head and a look in its eye that Acharon could only describe as intelligent. In his mind he was sure the dog was trying to determine how it could get inside. Acharon wasn't going to let that happen.

He kept the shotgun aimed on the dog as the gate slowly reached the ground and sealed them inside. When the gate motor whined to a stop he lowered the shotgun. His hands shook with excess adrenaline.

"Is it safe?" asked Sovelet.

Acharon watched the dog through the horizontal steel bars of the gate. On the other side of the gate Acharon knew there was another red button. If it were pressed, the gate would rise and the dogs would get in.

"I won't feel safe until we're inside the building." And something was wedged against the door.

08

"You think they'll get in?" Sovelet stood back while Acharon adjusted the chair.

"No."

He'd grabbed the chair nearest the door the moment he'd stepped through behind Sovelet. He'd dropped everything else and wedged the chair under the door handle so that no one, or no thing, could push the handle down. While he hopefully doubted the large dog could get the roll door open, he felt it better to take some simple precautions to make sure that was as far as the dog did get.

Through the window that made up most of the top half of the door, he watched the dogs milling around beyond the roll-up. Some seemed eager, jumping at the door or barking at it. Others seemed bored, licking themselves or lying on the dirt layered drive and closing their eyes. Only one seemed to be focused. The large dog had sniffed along the bottom of the door and the area where Acharon had stood while the door came down. What could it learn? It didn't see the button Acharon had pushed. But what if it could smell it?

Acharon shivered at the thought. He turned and flashed a weak smile at Sovelet and gathered up the shotgun and duffel bag. He turned to face the room. They hadn't been here in years. From the smell of dust and mildew, no one had.

Like many medical facilities from the days when thousands of patients had to be served, the medi-facs had waiting rooms. Acharon and Sovelet had come through this emergency admittance facility before, though he barely remembered the first time. There was the usual seating section and then the admittance counter. Where once nurses had stood to take information there were touch screen panels instead. As the population had decreased, the panels did all the admitting and then directed the patient to a medi-pod of the appropriate level. In dire emergencies, if the patient had not already arrived in a field emergency pod, they would be directed to lie in one at that time. The field-pods could maintain a person by pumping blood or oxygen, provide pain relief, or induce a medical coma to keep the person alive while being delivered to an appropriate medi-pod for treatment.

Fifty years ago, Sovelet would have come here or to the general admittance area and explained to the touchscreen what the problem was. She would have then been sent for a second opinion examination at one of the pods on this level. Once the diagnosis had been confirmed, she would have been whisked up to the fifth floor. There the full-capability medi-pods would have removed her lungs, printed new ones, and put her back together. From there she'd have been shuttled to a recovery room where, after spending half a day recovering, she'd have been up and good as new.

But nothing in the admittance rooms worked. They'd been turned off when the population had gone below a thousand. From that point, most people used the medi-pods at the enclave. There were a few rest stops through the city, but those medi-pods could do only as much as set a bone or staple a wound closed. For serious work, a person would have to endure the enclave or come here. There was one medi-pod at the enclave that could do organ replacement. So, if there was some catastrophe that required two or more people to have organ replacement immediately, the others would come here.

Or, as was Acharon's situation, if a person couldn't expect safe treatment at the enclave, they could always come here. Even though the admittance screens were off, each floor's medi-pods, each of increasing complexity from annual physicals up to organ replacement, still worked. Or they should work.

"Elevator?"

"Hopefully," Acharon said. He looked around, reorienting himself and then went to the right.

With Sovelet close on his heels they went around a corner and down a hall that terminated at a set of elevator doors. He pushed the up button and the light flicked on.

"Button works."

In a few seconds, as the sleeping systems booted back to life, they heard the whir and clink of gears as the elevator crawled down to the first floor. There were no cables to break or hydraulics to leak in these elevators. Gears propelled the elevator upward. In much taller buildings the same elevators could move sideways as well.

"Here we are," Acharon said as the elevator doors opened with a muffled screech.

Sovelet entered and Acharon followed. He turned and pushed the button for floor five, major surgery pods. He kept his eyes on the hall and his finger near the shotgun's trigger until the doors groaned closed and the elevator jolted upward. Only then did he relax.

"They got to you. The dogs."

Acharon shrugged and smiled sheepishly. "That's not an experience I'd care to repeat."

"They could be waiting for us when we leave."

"I've thought about that," Acharon said. "We might be able to use the monorail. It runs through the second level."

"And through the enclave," Sovelet said. She raised her eyebrows at him, reminding him that he didn't like to go there. "And the monorail is busted on Market. We'd have to get out a stop earlier and walk?"

"We could go toward the enclave. Just not all the way. There's several garages that the monorail passes near. Might find a car still attached to a charge. Drive the rest of the way. It'd take longer since we'd have to switch tracks."

"Maybe."

Acharon nodded in agreement. "Maybe. But let's get through this first and then we'll worry about what happens next."

The doors on the elevator opened as Acharon finished talking, as if signaling agreement with him. He smiled and waved Sovelet through. He was no longer concerned about dogs since they couldn't get to this level. Now his attention was focused on Sovelet and getting her well.

They walked down the short hallway and turned to their right.

They were standing in the exact same position as the first floor, but instead of an admittance desk the room they stood in was larger, emptier. There was a nurse's station in the center and six doors on the three walls around the station. These were the major surgery medi-pod rooms. Acharon's first memories of the place were filled with anger, blood, and pain.

"Room three?" Sovelet asked.

"Family tradition? Sure, why not."

They opened the door to room three. Acharon ignored the dried bloodstains that marked a meandering trail to the pod's door. The bots had cleaned the room, but some stains were more stubborn.

As they stepped into the room, the lights faded on, revealing the large mass of the medi-pod. The one in Sausalito that did diagnostics and basic medical treatment was the size of a mini-van. The major surgery medi-pods were the size of a mid-size moving van and nearly as tall. Tall enough that floor six had to be incorporated to hold their volume. But they could do anything. Acharon knew this firsthand and was glad for it.

A disagreement between factions at the San Francisco enclave had cost him an eye and almost his life. Decisive action on the part of Sovelet and several others caught in the middle of the schism had made the difference. They'd bundled him into a monorail pod and got him to the medi-fac as quickly as technology would allow. He'd phased in and out of consciousness, not sure if he was going to live. There was so much pain that when he'd felt a blackness enveloping him he'd grabbed at it willingly. Several hours later he'd woken in a recovery room, sporting a brand new eye that looked no different from the one that had been pierced with the penknife Thyme had been holding.

"Hey, you," Sovelet said. She'd punched him in the arm for emphasis. "I'm the one that's supposed to be nervous."

"You'll be fine. Trust me. I've been there. Right there." He pointed to the shiny white plastic surgery table inside the medi-pod. When the machine started running, electrodes would warm the plastic to body temperature and the circulating air would be the exact temperature to make the body feel most comfortable.

"You sure it's going to run?"

"The elevator worked," Acharon said. He laid the shotgun, backpack, and duffel bag on a counter by the chair. "And this was given more attention than that."

He located the operating system touchscreen and tapped it. The touchscreen flickered once and then a small rotating globe appeared in the middle.

"There you are," Acharon said. Just needs to warm up and we'll be good to go."

They both stood patiently before the touchscreen and waited as the little globe spun. It spun for several minutes. Just as Acharon was starting to get nervous, the screen blinked and a message window appeared.

"'Not enough power for full operational ability.' What do we do?"

Acharon had to think for a bit. Like the warehouses, the roofs of the medi-fac buildings were covered with solar panels. They should have been self-cleaning here. But maybe the systems had failed. He didn't like that thought since he was partially responsible for them. But if they were working, perhaps power was being drawn off by other systems. What other systems would be running?

Nothing except the few lights, the elevator, and now the medi-pod. They should be the only things needing energy.

He laughed as he realized his own foolishness.

"What's so funny?" Sovelet asked.

"Me," Acharon said. "I was trying to figure out what could be wrong. And it's me."

"You? You lost me on this one, Ach."

"The wind turbines on the roofs. They have a lockdown mode that they slip into when they aren't needed to produce power."

"It was windy enough outside," Sovelet said.

"You're right. But the lockdown has a mechanical element. They have to be released manually. Will you be okay here alone?"

"Why? Where are you going?"

Acharon went to his duffel bag and rummaged out a pair of thick microfiber gloves.

"I have to go on the roof. You can come with me, but it'd be faster if I just went."

Sovelet looked around the room. Acharon watched as her gaze drifted across the reclining chair she'd used once before while waiting for Acharon's new eye to be printed and installed. But she only moved once she noticed the computer terminal on the wall.

"I can wait," she said.

"Great." Acharon went to the door and looked at the handle. No lock. "We should find something to wedge under here until I get back."

"The dogs aren't going to get up here, Ach. Just go and hurry back."

"Fine, but keep the shotgun close." He pulled a .45 handgun from his backpack. "Couple minutes and I'll be back."

"Go already!" Sovelet made a show of picking up the shotgun and carrying it over to the terminal.

Acharon opened the door and slipped past, closing it behind him. The nurses' station was gloomily lit by windows on the fourth wall, the one facing Parnassus. Acharon took a few seconds to look out and down. He could see only the outer edge of the courtyard and the entrance. He did not see any dogs. He wasn't sure if that was a good thing or a bad thing. He had to hope that it was a good thing.

There were eight floors in the building and the elevator groaned its way up. Once there he meandered a bit until remembering where to find the service access to the roof.

The solar cells on the medi-fac weren't as badly blocked with guano and debris. They looked pretty good, in Acharon's opinion, for cells left to fend for themselves for decades. It also looked like most of them had their cleaning apparatuses still intact. The cleaning apparatuses were two armed windshield wipers. Instead of sweeping an arc that missed twenty percent of the available surface, these wipers were pulled from the top to the bottom, acting like a full-surface squeegee. They cleared ninety-five percent of the surface, sacrificing the edges which were more frame than solar cell. It was good to see something still working as it was supposed to work.

Near the four corners of the roof were four vertical wind turbines. Unlike the traditional windmill style, these had vertical blades that connected at the tops and bottoms with a twist in the middle that caught the wind. These took up less space and proved to be less dangerous for birds. All four of them stood motionless.

As Acharon had predicted, the manual locks on the turbines had dropped into place. This kept the turbines from spinning and wearing themselves out uselessly. The manual lock was a magnetic release collar that dropped and locked the spinning tower against the stationary base column. All Acharon had to do was lift the collars and reposition the magnets that held the collars until once again the turbines weren't needed.

This turned out to be more work than he'd hoped. The years had been gentle but still inconsiderate to simplification. Debris, always the debris, had worked its way into the space between collar and column, making it almost impossible to move. The fading daylight didn't help, either. Acharon had to work at the collar, twisting it left and right, then pulling upward and shoving down. Dirt slipped through as he attacked the stubborn metal. About the time he considered taking a break and employing a different tactic involving a hammer and some choice language, the first collar popped up.

Acharon quickly reset the collar support magnets. He then opened a box connected to the turbine and pushed a stubborn button to reset the turbine's system. After the reset, he closed the box and stepped back and waited.

Slowly at first, the first turbine began to move. There was a chorus of scratching and grinding noises as debris was ground away. The blades began to turn more easily with each additional rotation. The breeze coaxed them on and they spun faster and faster until they were spinning at maximum rotation for the current winds.

Satisfied with the turbine's motion, Acharon turned and looked at the remaining three. It was a lot of work, but he wanted to make sure that the medi-pod had all the energy it needed. He heaved a sigh and moved to the second turbine.

Now that he knew what to do, freeing the other three turbines went more smoothly. Soon enough, three of the turbines spun smoothly. The fourth was clear and reset but still wouldn't spin. Three would have to be enough.

Smelling like a statue that had seen too many pigeons, sweating and thirsty, he found himself pausing on his way to the roof access. He was standing at the edge of the roof, looking across the western part of the city. The day had dimmed to mid-sunset. He could see the sun playing a game of peek-a-boo behind striations of clouds low on the horizon.

Living in Sausalito meant they seldom saw the sun settle down over the horizon. Their evenings always came a few hours earlier as the hill shadows tucked them in for the evening.

When was the last time anyone had seen the sun set off the coast of California? Had it been years? And was this the last time? Was this his last time? Based on his last two medical exams, he had the potential for another fifty years of life. Would he see the sunset again? If the sun set and there wasn't anyone to witness it, did it really happen?

He chuckled at the thought. He was definitely tired. Hungry and tired. And there was still more to be done.

By the time Acharon exited the elevator on the fifth floor his stomach had begun to register its displeasure. So not only was he tired and smelly, his stomach was twisting in hunger, his arms quivered from the lack of energy and his exertion up on the roof. But three of the turbines were spinning properly. The lights in the nurses' station now glowed brightly, and gentle muzak drifted from the ceiling speakers. Except for the absence of nurses, doctors, and patients it almost felt as if he'd gone back in time.

He knocked on the door to room three before entering. Computer code drifted up the terminal screen as he entered the room, but Sovelet wasn't at the station. Sometime between her doing something on the computer and his return, she had fallen asleep in the chair, her head tilted against its back. Her breathing came in short, rapid breaths. Her face was pale. He wanted to wake her and let her know she could get in the medi-pod now. At the same time, he wanted to watch her sleeping peacefully. Well, mostly peaceful. For nearly a hundred years he'd woken in the middle of the night, nearly every night. He always tried to go back to sleep. When he couldn't, he'd turn toward Sovelet and just watch her breathing deeply, her face relaxed. Sometimes there'd be the hint of a Mona Lisa smile on her lips. The next thing he'd know it would be morning and she would be watching him, her smile much more pronounced.

He let her sleep. The computers in the medi-pod needed a few minutes more to come fully awake. He would let her sleep that long at least. The afternoon had been scary and she was probably worn out from the adrenaline and difficulty breathing.

He went to the medi-pod and touched the screen. This time the little globe spun faster and then quickly expanded to reveal the medical screen. Acharon began entering information. He could tell the computer to access the medi-pod in Sausalito and give it Sovelet's recent data. It would also access and collate the entirety of her medical history wherever it was stored or entered. All of that assumed that the lines of communication to all the databases were still open.

It took several more minutes for the system to catch up. Acharon turned to watch Sovelet several times before turning back to check the computer screen. Eventually there was a soft chime and the screen flashed green. The entrance to the medi-pod lifted. It was time.

Acharon went to the chair where Sovelet slept and gently put a hand on her forearm. Her eyes opened slowly, dreamily, and she smiled when their eyes met.

"Hey," she said.

"Hey."

Sovelet lifted her head. She looked around, her eyes coming to a stop when she saw the open medi-pod.

"You got it working."

"Of course I did." He helped her to her feet. "I've entered all the data. It found everything it needs and is ready to go."

"All I have to do is step in."

"Unless you're hungry." He smiled.

Sovelet looked confused. She rubbed her face with the palm of a hand before going to the terminal and shutting down the program she had on the screen. "Hungry? Why?"

"Well, I'm hungry," Acharon said. He held out a hand and helped her stand. "So, if you want, we could go down to three, to the canteen, and see what magic the food machines can perform."

"Or we could just get this over with. I won't know I'm hungry when I'm asleep."

"That's true." He paused. "So you're ready?"

She nodded and they moved together toward the open door of the medi-pod. She paused at the entrance and turned toward him. Her hand rubbed gently on his chest.

"We've lived so long already, Ach."

He took her hand and gently squeezed. "We've got longer to live. Please."

"Why do we go on living, Ach? Have you given it any thought? We don't reproduce. That's the primary mission of any living creature: propagate the species. If we're not doing that, what's the point?"

"I don't have an answer. Maybe I will when your surgery is done and I've had a chance to eat. Maybe take a shower. I'll think of something to say. I promise. But for now?"

He indicated the waiting medi-pod with the tilt of his head.

"Well, maybe I'll feel different when I can breathe better." She stepped across the threshold, moving more like a twenty-first-century centenarian than a modern sesquitarian.

"I'm betting on it," Acharon said.

"I won't be long," Sovelet said. She kissed Acharon on the lips and then entered the pod. She touched the screen next to the surgery bed and the door came down like a slow motion trap.

The bottom two thirds of the glass walls went opaque. Acharon watched Sovelet's head moving as she slowly undressed. She looked in his direction several times and smiled. Quickly enough, she disappeared from view when she lay on the table. After a few seconds the walls shifted back to clear. Surgery barriers had risen around the table. Only Sovelet's head was visible.

She turned and smiled once more at Acharon.

Her smile always initiated an ache in his chest. Normally it was from the weight of his love for her. Now, it was the weight of his fear for her, and his fear for himself. He hid it all behind a wave and a smile.

She winked at him as the respirator slowly descended along with a hypodermic arm. The mask covered her face and the hypodermic initiated a sedative injection. Sovelet's eyes slowly drifted shut.

Now there was just the waiting. He could do that here. He could pace or try to sleep. He paused as his stomach growled its frustration.

Or he could eat.

09

In no time since the day he was born had Acharon felt so alone as he did now. An island to himself in a sea of empty tables and white plastic chairs. Bright lights of the canteen accentuating his isolation by obliterating every shadow the moment he'd entered.

The isolation hadn't hit him right away. It was only after he'd started to order for two and realized there was only one to dine did it finally register. Mutely, an ache in his chest, he collected his meal for one and carried it to a table against a wall. He sat with the wall behind him, its presence more a comfort than the open space before him.

Was this how it would one day be? Would he one day dine alone all the time? Worse yet, would Sovelet have to dine alone? For as long as he knew her, Acharon had never dined alone. They had never dined alone. Certainly, they may have eaten separately, in different parts of the city or him in Sausalito, she on their island, but they would talk on the radios while they ate. Apart, but never separated. Never alone.

There was no radio that could bring her to him right now. Not while she slept and the machines built and placed new lungs in her chest. But this was a reminder of how things could be.

Acharon pushed the sweet potato mash with his spoon, occasionally remembering to put some in his mouth. His mind wandered back to yesterday. It had been only yesterday, but it felt like ages. Finding Murphy and his note. Had Murphy been feeling this way? Dining alone for decades until he just got tired of meals for one? Could he do it? If Sovelet died and he was alone for ten, twenty years, could he just push the stop button? Sovelet might be able to. She hadn't said it, but he was sure that she thought about it.

Thinking of her, dead, killed the remainder of his appetite. He fed the tray into the recycler and added the cup after downing the last of the coffee that had cooled while he'd mulled over what might be.

He'd go back upstairs. Being in the same room would help his mood. Knowing that very soon she would be up and about and they could be on their way back to their island buoyed his mood. As for the dogs? With Sovelet with him, he was sure that would be easy to solve, too.

Memories of their long life soothed his ache as he waited for the elevator to carry him up to the fifth floor. The memories froze as the doors opened and he heard the muffled klaxon of alarm bells.

In the waiting area he spun around, looking for the source of the alarm. He knew what he feared but clung to the hope he was wrong. The nurses' station computers were asleep and provided no clue. He didn't want to go into room three. If he didn't go, it couldn't be happening.

But if he didn't go, he wouldn't know what was happening. He moved to the door and shoved it open. The alarm's volume increased without the door to muffle the sound. There was no denying the situation now.

He rushed to the medi-pod, planting his hands against the glass, looking for Sovelet's face. His breath blew a pulsating circle of condensation in quarter-time to his rapidly beating heart.

Sovelet still lay on the surgery table. Her body was hidden by the courtesy screen but he could see her face and the respirator still hugging her mouth and nose. The surgical arms appeared frozen in mid-motion. How long had the klaxons been sounding?

Acharon moved to the touchscreen and pressed for vital signs. He sighed with relief as he took in the information that assured him that she was still alive. So what was the problem? He scanned the screen, looking for some indicator that would guide him to the answer. Looking for something that would give him a problem to solve.

On the bottom of the screen a word flashed: Organics.

Organics were the containers of elements and compounds that were used to print everything from medications to the organs used in transplants. Each organ was printed with the patient's DNA as a base of construction so that the organs were never rejected. The organics were stored in long tubes in the back of the medi-pod.

Acharon stepped quickly around the medi-pod to an access door on the back. Beyond the door were more panels for items like surgical sterilizers, bandage printers, computer interfaces, and the organics tubes. The panel for the organics had four knobbed bolts that could be unscrewed by hand.

Acharon quickly spun the bolts off and pulled the panel aside. There were three organics tube receptacles. All of them were empty. They shouldn't be. There wasn't any reason for them to be empty. They contained enough material to reprint every organ in a person three times over. Even if the containers had gone empty, there was an automatic loader to replace the empty containers. That was so no one found themselves in Sovelet's position, lying on a table, in the middle of a surgery, suspended between life and death. The machines couldn't actually put back the old organ once it had been removed.

A panel above the first held the reload canisters. Acharon undid the knobs and pulled it off.

It was empty.

Acharon stepped back, confused. The system held thirty-six canisters in reserve. They should have all been here, stacked up like cans of soda in a vending machine. But there was nothing.

Why would they be gone? The supply of containers was enough to last thousands of people hundreds of years. They couldn't have run out of them.

Another machine.

With the klaxons as chorus to his urgency, Acharon rushed out of the room and banged the door open on room two. Quicker than the first time he was inside the medi-pod and opening the access panel to the organics.

Nothing. Acharon swore and fumbled the knobs off the access to the reload canisters. Also empty. Acharon slammed his way out of room two and into room one.

The medi-pod in room one was also missing its entire stock of organics canisters. As was room four where he went next.

The same empty chambers greeted him in room five. Acharon's

head hurt with confusion and the rage of the klaxons still blaring from room three. It affected his concentration and he almost missed something that was where the canisters should have been.

Words on a torn square of paper that had been taped to the back of the organics chamber. A fear chilled Acharon and he tore the paper off the wall and read it.

Anyone needing these containers knows where to get them, it read. And it was signed by Thyme.

"Shit," Acharon said. His eye ached at the recollection.

When the entire population of San Francisco was small enough to fit into the enclave, the trouble slowly began. The original intent and design of the enclaves was to allow each person to live their life as they chose. There weren't any plans for people to assume roles of leadership that allowed them to control others. These were the last of humanity. They didn't want any of them to be subservient to any other.

While every effort was made to avoid the word, the enclaves were established to exist as communes. Everyone was to share equally in everything, including decisions concerning the enclave's actions.

However, as seems often to be the fate of mankind, where there is an opportunity for someone to grab power, there's someone who wants to grab. Thyme, with several followers, had made that grab for power.

Thyme's ascension went with hardly anyone noticing or caring. Most of the members of the enclave didn't care what power Thyme granted himself just so long as he didn't interfere with their lives as they were interested in living them.

So Thyme became the self-proclaimed leader of the San Francisco enclave. At first life went along as it had before. It was only after the Oakland enclave fire, when some of the survivors had come across to San Francisco, that things began to turn ugly. Thyme began creating rules. These rules controlled access to supplies and where and how people went about in the city. He did all this with the help of a squad of cronies and the complacency of the rest of the people of the enclave.

Even Acharon hadn't thought much of Thyme's actions then. He had his own priorities. Those priorities were Sovelet's happiness and maintenance checks on any and every system he encountered. He knew that their lives, or at least their comfortable lives, depended on the machinery of their shrinking society. He was intent on keeping as much of it working until the last human gave up their last breath.

It was the wall around the enclave that had finally riled its residents. Then came the treatment of the Oakland refugees. It was after that, long after Thyme's control of the enclave had solidified, that the rest of the community protested in a full meeting. It was there that Acharon had stood up against Thyme. It was that altercation that cost him his eye.

It had been a heated exchange of words. But that was all anyone was expecting. Shouting and throwing arms up in frustration were standard actions for these meetings. No one, least of all Acharon, suspected Thyme was palming a penknife. No one realized how willing or eager Thyme was to use it.

After coming to the medi-fac center and having a new eye made, Acharon and Sovelet did not return to the enclave. They spent a few days holing up in a home in the Marina district until they developed the plan for their own island.

They'd never returned to the enclave after that.

Now he had to return. A place that he'd sworn never to return to, he now had to go. There wasn't another alternative.

He closed the panels and shut the access door and returned to room three. Sovelet still lay unconscious on the operating platform. She looked relaxed. According to the screen, the machines were breathing for her. They couldn't do that for long. According to the readings, in seventeen hours and fifty minutes there would be problems with bleeding and oxygen levels.

Acharon wasn't going to let her lie there that long.

"I have to run an errand," he said. His voice was loud, to be heard through the glass, even though he knew she couldn't hear. "I'll be back shortly." He patted the plastic wall. "Don't go anywhere."

He went to the counter and loaded up his pack with supplies from the duffel bag. He took rope, collapsible bolt cutters, rounds for the shotgun and the .45, two high-powered flashlights, and some of the protein bars that were always kept in an outer pocket. Last he grabbed the gloves he'd worn on the roof. After a final check on Sovelet and her status, he left the room and headed to the elevator.

When they began building the monorail system they decided, for reasons not shared with Acharon, to place stations in some of the buildings. Perhaps this gave the system a futuristic appeal, a la Disneyland. It had been a headache to design and implement. Acharon had been on one of the early teams that helped with the design of the carriages and their power system. They'd designed the carriages with solar cell skins, so that when they sat in or moved through the daylight, they utilized the solar power or stored it for the evenings. But how would they get sunlight if they were left for long periods in the building stations?

Only now was Acharon glad that they'd solved the problem.

The elevator doors opened onto the second floor. Had it been the middle of the day, Acharon would have been dazzled by the bright daylight funneled and magnified through light tunnels bringing light down from the roof. The light tunnels could magnify weak light and make it seem as if the sun was in full glory at high noon. Even on a day covered in fog or dense clouds the station would be awash with bright light.

There were seven carriages waiting at the station. Four were on the clockwise track, three on the counterclockwise. Being inside, Acharon was confident that these would run even after a fifty-year hiatus. He pressed the access panel for the front carriage of the clockwise track, which still had its numbers clearly visible under a skin of dust, and the panel lit. He punched a code and the doors slid silently open as if they'd just been assembled that morning.

From the inside, he could see through a clean and clear window. The touchscreen responded immediately and he tapped his finger on the enclave's circle as his destination. The doors slid silently together and the pod moved forward with a gentle thrust.

The doors that blocked the exit from the building were less cooperative. The carriage had to stop completely and wait as the doors grudgingly swung outward. When they'd parted the minimum allowed space, the carriage moved slowly through a shower of dirt and leaves until it cleared the building. It left the bright light of the station behind and entered the sharp darkness of a cloudless night.

Free of the building, the carriage increased its speed along the track, turning left and then diving down toward Golden Gate Park. As they crossed Parnassus, Acharon looked back to the medi-fac. The exterior lights were on in the courtyard where they'd left the dogs. Where at least one dog had been examining the drop-down gate. He wasn't sure what he was hoping to see. He didn't know if not seeing the dogs was good or bad. They could still be in the courtyard, they could have gotten distracted by other prey, or they could have gotten into the building. If they were in the building, Sovelet was safe; it would just make his journey back a little more complicated.

The monorail track Acharon's carriage rode on dashed to California Street. California Street was a major interchange for the monorails. Most of the buildings in a block radius of California and Arguello had been torn down to handle the network of switches for the monorail system. From here the lines shot out to the Golden Gate Bridge which it no longer crossed because of the collapsed span, west to run along Highway One, and the one his carriage was switching over to that would take him east to the enclave at Huntington Park.

The carriage slowed as it worked its way through the switches. Acharon could feel the vibrations as the tracks switched with aged effort, banging into their new positions. The carriage wiggled its way through and once it was on the straight track east, its speed picked up.

None of this was happening fast enough for Acharon. If he thought it would have helped, he would have pushed the carriage or held his breath or whistled. Anything to make it go faster. But there was nothing he could do. The carriage was going as fast as was safe, based on specifications that he'd help to design and the conditions of the rail. All he could do was try to remain calm, accepting what he could not change.

He tried distracting himself from his frustration by watching the city. It passed by as brief highlights in the dark. Most of it was sharp lines and hard angles. In a few places, the lines were rounder and softer. These were places where buildings were absent, nature present.

Some of these were open areas that had not been there when the first of the Last Wavers were being born. When Acharon and Sovelet were still in diapers, many governments had gotten it into their heads to remove buildings and homes as they became vacant from a dwindling population. It took a while for a counter movement to build momentum.

It was eventually decided that as much of humanity's presence on Earth should be preserved as was possible. Perhaps aliens from another planet might find them. Perhaps another earth species might rise to the levels of humanity and discover the ruins of a past civilization of an extinct species. It was, some agreed, a desperate grasp at extending the history of humanity. It was a straw that many agreeably grasped with eager hands.

That was when they developed the plastic coating used to preserve many buildings along with national monuments and landmarks. Many of the skyscrapers in the financial district had the coating as well as the government buildings and historical structures. But even that was no guarantee. The collapsed building that took out the monorail on Market was evidence of that truth.

Acharon had thought the removal of a lot of the old structures was a good idea. They created green belts that encouraged fauna to enter the towns and cities. To think that nature would respect humanity's efforts was foolhardy. As was hoping there would be something left to remind the future of humanity's passing.

It all seemed pretty arrogant to Acharon. Humanity had its run and committed suicide along the way. Let the next species puzzle over the bones like humans did with dinosaurs.

The carriage began to slow. Acharon looked up in surprise. The enclave was still blocks away. The carriage was still on the steep slope that wouldn't tail off until it passed Grace Cathedral. The monorail station was directly in front of the old Pacific Union Club, Thyme's command center.

Acharon stood and moved to the front of the carriage. He held onto the overhead support rail as he leaned forward to see the reason for the carriage's reduced speed. He hoped that it wasn't another break in the rails. If it was, he'd have to back the carriage to Van Ness and hike back up.

In a few more seconds the carriage's headlights illuminated the problem. The carriage slowed to a stop.

When Acharon and Sovelet had left the city for good, there'd been a wall that encircled the enclave. Thyme's wall. It had been made of steel plates and one-ton cement blocks scavenged from the old industrial areas and stacked across streets and alleys. The wall reached from building to building, blocking off all access to the enclave except where the monorail crossed through. The wall had been twenty feet high in most places by the time the schism had reached its boiling point.

Apparently there'd been additional improvements after Acharon had left. In the dim light from the carriage he could see that the wall now blocked off California Street. Steel gates reached around and over the carriage's track.

The carriage had stopped fifty feet from the steel gates. Rust streaks stained the gates and faded stencils forbade any admittance. To the left and right short towers of scaffolding peeked over the top of the wall, paranoid with wraps of razor wire. There was a narrow gap between the two gate doors. A lone light in the enclave backlit three dark lines across the gap, suggesting the presence of crossbars holding the gate shut.

Acharon shook his head. How bad had things gotten after he and Sovelet had left? What did Thyme and those who'd stayed in the enclave have to fear? There were no more armies on the planet unless you took into account ants and other insects. The dogs, back when Acharon had left with a bloody compress over his eye, hadn't gathered together as they appeared to be doing now.

Was this just paranoia? Sullen pouting that required some sort of statement of hurt?

Whatever it was, it was making Acharon's errand complicated.

He went to the touchscreen and accessed the emergency menus. He entered his access code, glad that he'd kept it simple, and directed the carriage to open its doors.

The carriage complied silently. Only a puff of breeze across his neck indicated that the doors had opened.

Acharon pulled out a flashlight and turned it on before climbing down onto the narrow platform that the monorail track was supported on. Since there would never be anyone to come and rescue stranded passengers, the designers had made the monorail track with a wide base that could be used as an emergency walkway. A narrow rail along the sides allowed for some modicum of safety for a person trying to move to the front or rear of the carriage.

Once in front of the carriage, Acharon made his way along the walkway toward the gates using the flashlight as a guide. Sovelet had doubted that anyone was left. She hadn't seen any electronic evidence indicative of human presence. But that didn't mean no one was alive. There could be some, like Thyme, who avoided the Internet with a paranoid mania. Even now they could be watching him and wondering what he was up to.

He came to a stop about five meters from the gates. He held his arms out to his sides. He had nothing to hide. The flashlight beam cut a cone of light into the sky as he held it pointing up. He called out, "Hello?"

When there was no response he tried louder, shouting his greeting. "Hello!"

His voice echoed across the silence of the city.

Again, after no response he was sure of only one thing: no one was answering at the gate. It didn't mean someone wasn't inside, ignoring him or unaware of him. He'd have to get in to find out.

There had obviously been changes to Thyme's wall. Acharon considered this as he slipped back into the carriage and grabbed his pack and shotgun. He needed to find a way down. Once there he knew of several buildings on Clay Street where, if there hadn't been too much hardening of the defenses, he could find entrance. But first he had to get down.

There were emergency stairs along the monorail route but they were at the platforms. The nearest one was on the other side of the enclave gate. Perhaps there were other options.

Once he began to study his options for descent, they began to look bleak. He'd checked along the gate, thinking maybe they'd cut in handholds for themselves, or at least left a ladder behind. None of that hadn't happened and he was considering taking the carriage back to the last station and looking for a car or just hiking back up to the enclave. But while he mulled over his options he played his flashlight's beam around and over the monorail track and its walkway and saw his solution.

In the circle of light from the flashlight, Acharon could see that four produce trucks were sitting beneath the monorail track and lined up in front of the gate. They looked like they'd arrived long ago, only to be denied access to the enclave. Their tops were liberally coated with guano and islands of moss growing in a mottled pattern. Their tires looked flat from years of standing still. Flat tires affected the height, but the trucks still reduced the drop to ten feet. The rope was going to come in handy.

Acharon looped the rope through the track's railing and dropped the ends to the top of the last truck. He lowered himself the short distance to the truck's refrigerator box roof and then pulled one end of the rope until he had all of it back. He then coiled the rope and stowed it in his pack.

It was a short drop from the refrigerator box to the cab roof, then a short drop to the hood, the wheel fender, and finally the ground. The closer he got to the ground the more earthy a smell he detected. It seemed that the trucks having arrived laden with fresh produce and been denied entrance had then remained waiting until the batteries died and all the vegetables inside composted. The stench must have been worse the first few months. It was surprising that no one had let the trucks enter or at least ventured out to acquire some of the vegetables.

Around him, the only signs of life were a few muted bird chirps and a rustling as something moved from one branch to another. Random bugs hummed past, attracted by the flashlight's illumination. Other than that, it was quiet.

It was a quiet that pleased him and made him uncomfortable at the same time. They'd seen plenty of wildlife besides the dogs on the drive to the medi-fac but nothing now. It might mean nothing, being so late in the evening, but then it might mean something. Perhaps all the other animals were making themselves scarce, like townsfolk before the showdown at high noon, or high midnight in this case. He checked the shotgun once again. Better to be prepared. It had served him well so far.

He gave one last look to the gated monorail track. He ran the beam of the flashlight across its surface, wishfully hoping for a secret entrance to show itself. Once satisfied that nothing of the sort was going to happen, he started walking up Jones toward Sacramento. He held the shotgun in his right hand, the barrel resting across the crook of his left. He slowly swung the flashlight left and right as he walked. His finger rested along the side of the trigger. When he was finally inside the enclave he'd stop worrying about dogs. Though there still might be a bigger danger waiting there.

10

By the time Acharon reached the corner of Sacramento and Jones he still hadn't seen or heard anything more than an owl in the distance and the bugs entranced by his flashlight beam. He spent several minutes with his head cocked to one side, attempting to pull in any stray sound. In the far distance he could just hear the whisper of the ocean battering the shore on the other side of the Great Highway. Hearing nothing of relevance for the moment, he shrugged off his disquiet and continued walking.

At the corner of Jones and Clay he turned his attention to the five-story apartment building that marked the northwest corner of the enclave.

The steel and cement block wall that had denied him access to the enclave monorail station ran along the back of Grace Cathedral, crossed Sacramento Avenue, and butted up against the corner of the condo building that marked the southwest corner of the enclave.

Here, on the other side of Sacramento Avenue, all the way down Jones Street and to Pleasant, the doors and windows on the first floors and the windows on the second floors had been plated with slabs of steel, the kind once used to covered potholes and ditches cut into roads. Large, taunting eyebolts stuck out on the street side. Inside, from past experience, he knew there was another piece of metal impaled on the eye bolt and secured by a fist-sized nut. There was no removing the plates except from the inside or with the help of a very large bulldozer that would also remove most of the wall. Unfortunately, he didn't have immediate access to a bulldozer.

There were other options, of course. But moving on to each option took more time. The more time he was running around searching for a way in, the more time ticked away on Sovelet's clock. It was his firm hope that the Clay Street side of the corner building had held tight to its recent past.

In the early days of the enclave, before the hotels around Huntington Park were being converted into condominiums, many of the Last Wavers had begun to settle in nearby apartments. For many, even after the more technically advanced homes had been finished, it was easier to just stay in the old places. The building on the corner of Jones and Clay was just such a one.

So when the schism came and many bent to Thyme's will, those who didn't stayed to the edges of the enclave, in the older apartments. This kept them far from the center of Thyme's locus of control, out of sight and mostly out of Thyme's mind. Acharon and Sovelet had come often to this apartment building to visit with like-minded people. People who often wondered why Acharon and Sovelet didn't just move into the building. There were plenty of apartments still unoccupied. But if he had, who would have stood up for those being pushed around by Thyme and his bully brigade?

And if he had, would he have never lost his eye? Would they still be the last ones left?

The memories cascaded to the forefront of Acharon's thoughts, dazing him into a stillness. His eyes searched the windows, recalling good times in a dark period. There'd been many days and nights spent playing cards, watching old movies, and generally being in pleasant company. The apartments had become the hub of anarchists and independents.

Acharon was hoping that those same feelings and attitudes from the past were going to work in his favor in the present. He only had to turn down Clay Street to discover if it was so.

Along the Clay side of the building were two garage entrances. Many of the Last Wavers that had chosen to live in the building had continued their independence with personal cars. Acharon had helped add the solar panels and turbines to the roof of the building and along the roofs of adjacent buildings. When the schism began, he and several others had made the building's system independent of the rest of the enclave's power grid. This took away part of Thyme's system of control as he couldn't punish the residents by taking away their electricity.

The garage doors had been wired to the system, allowing people to continue to use the automatic garage door openers. Acharon didn't have a garage door remote for the building, but if they were still operational, there was a keypad by the door.

And, indeed, the garage doors were not blocked. His flashlight picked out broken pieces of concrete, strewn across the street along with several iron plates. Acharon got the impression that Thyme had tried and failed to control access to the building's garage. Unfortunately, his flashlight also illuminated an aged scar where someone had torn off the keypad.

What he needed now was a plan B. A plan anything would do as well. This was the best way into the enclave. So he needed to get one of the two garage doors open.

He turned the flashlight back to the rubble, looking for some kind of leverage. There was some rebar, but the pieces that were accessible were too small and the pieces he could have used had awkward chunks of cement attached to them. But there were cars. On the other side of the street, parked or pushed up onto the curb were a half dozen of them.

One he recognized from his days at the apartment building. It was an old Mercedes C-class. He recognized it because it was the car he and several of the others would go treasure hunting in. Sometimes they hunted for parts to fix things, sometimes they did it just for fun and curiosity. But whatever the reason, they always kept tools in the trunk. Crowbars, for example.

The doors were unlocked, just like most of the city, and he popped the trunk latch. In the trunk there was a box of old hardbound books, a crate with water and pre-packaged meals, and three crowbars. He had two hands, so he took two.

At the garage door Acharon set the flashlight down, pointing at the spot he was going to work at. He then shoved a crowbar tip under the garage door and pulled up on the bar. The door did not give to his efforts. It was going to take a little more work. He pushed the flat end of the second crowbar under the door to serve as a fulcrum for the first one, hoping that pushing down might leverage the door open.

He was just pushing the first crowbar under the door edge when he stopped. The hairs on the back of his neck stood, tingling. His back itched. Very slowly, he stood, bringing the crowbar with him. As he turned, the growling began.

It was a mixture of relief and from-frying-pan-to-fire emotions that twisted his gut and sweated his palms. He'd expected to find the dogs behind him, trapping him here. However, that turned out not to be the case. He was now facing three wolves.

Their teeth were bared. Their throaty growls had grown louder as he'd finally faced them. They were big. The alpha dog was of similar size, maybe a couple of centimeters taller, but big was big. Their hackles were raised, their heads low, and they were slowly separating, spreading out around him. Boxing Acharon in.

When he tried to slide his hand down to the handgun holster, the center wolf barked until Acharon ceased moving. It looked as though he was trapped. He found that despite his fear he was also feeling anger. The anger wasn't over his own demise but rather that he was leaving Sovelet without explanation, without her ever knowing anything. She'd lain down to have new lungs switched in for old ones, but would never know he'd failed her. He'd let her down and that was what made him the maddest, the angriest.

Despite the barking, Acharon lifted the crowbar with both hands. He'd go down swinging.

"Come on, you bastards." His words were his own growl of warning.

The wolf to his left lunged. Acharon swung down, as if he were driving an axe into wood. The wolf jerked back. Paranoid, Acharon took a one-armed swing to his right and caught the wolf coming in from that side. It yelped and sprang back.

The wolves retreated just out of crowbar reach. Acharon was sure that was the last contact he was going to make.

"Come on!" His shout was powered by fear and regret.

The wolves seemed to tense, ready to spring as one. Acharon swung the crowbar left to right and then back, a large arc with the hook of the crowbar point down. Maybe he would get one last lick in before they got to him. They'd remember.

Then there was chaos.

Noise came from everywhere. Barking echoed sharply off the walls, through the dark. It wasn't the throaty bark of the wolves, who'd suddenly turned from Acharon. It was dogs. A whole pack of them. They'd charged around the corner in silence and began barking as they rushed the wolves, much to Acharon's surprise. There wasn't any kind of hesitation he would have expected in a dog-wolf encounter. The dogs leapt, attacking as a pack.

The wolves fought back, snapping and tearing at the first dogs to reach them. They bunched together, leaving several bloody and wounded dogs on the road before them. They'd created a wall of raised fur and slowly backed away from the pack of dogs that had created their own wall, a half-dozen dogs wide and several deep.

Then there was more barking. Acharon was confused at first. He could see all the animals and none of them was barking. The barking was coming from somewhere else. Another pack from the other direction. More wolves? No, Acharon realized after a second of confusion, that was more dog barking.

The wolves seemed to recognize it, too. They leapt at the dogs in front of them. It looked as if they were trying to push and leap through the pack. Then the wolves were being attacked from all sides.

Acharon was mesmerized by the battle before him. So mesmerized that it took him a dozen heartbeats to realize that he'd been temporarily forgotten by the wolves and seemingly ignored by the dogs.

With his back to the garage door, he knelt and shoved the straight end of the crowbar back under the garage door. He had to look away once to shift the second bar so that it could again be the fulcrum. He stood after setting the crowbars and put one foot on the hooked end of the crowbar wedged under the door and pushed down.

The first push was disheartening as it didn't budge the door. A second effort, with the cries and barks of wolves and dogs as soundtrack, broke the garage door free from whatever had been holding it back.

Moving quickly, Acharon reversed the crowbar and hooked the door and pulled up. He had to turn his back to the battle and that action caused more sweat to flow than the effort of pulling the door up enough to slip under. He pushed the crowbars under, along with the flashlight. The flashlight spun and the light went out. He must have kicked it too hard in his eagerness to get away. There was nothing to be done for it now. He removed his pack and kicked it through the gap as well.

Now was the hard part. He watched the battle that the wolves seemed to be in the process of losing. One of them was already down, still being worried at by four of the smaller dogs. The window of time for escape was rapidly shutting. Acharon knelt as he watched the dogs. When it was clear he still wasn't on their radar, he threw himself prone and wiggled under the door.

With a held-breath gasp of relief, he jumped to his feet and felt for the garage door. He applied his weight to it, pulling it back down, closing the gap, and sealing himself off from the dogs. It came down grudgingly, making his heart race until it pressed against the concrete floor. He backed away from the door, breathing hard, and continued to listen to the sounds of the canine battle. There were fewer barks. Growls had diminished. Acharon had a pretty good gauge as to who was the loser.

The last barks were quickly being replaced by the snuffling of noses along the bottom of the garage door. Something banged against the door and Acharon flinched in surprise. There were several loud barks, more of the snuffling, and then nothing.

Acharon could imagine the dogs waiting quietly for him to get curious and stick his head out to see if they'd left. He wasn't that curious.

He took a few seconds to calm himself and catch his breath. Wolves and then the dogs. His body was shaking with another adrenaline rush. The only other thing that had ever affected him like this was the recurring nightmare of his eye being stabbed, over and over.

Once he felt calmer and could see a little in the dark of the garage, he pulled his backpack closer and felt around for the second flashlight.

He pulled out the flashlight. There was still the emergency flashlight in a small outer pocket but he would save that for a more dire emergency.

The question that Acharon had on his mind as he closed up the pack was, were the dogs that attacked the wolves the same dogs that had followed him and Sovelet to the medi-fac? He didn't believe it. Or, to be honest with himself, he didn't want to believe it. It didn't seem logical. But there was that twisting of his gut that suggested otherwise.

Quietly, when the snuffling along the door returned but he was satisfied that they wouldn't suddenly stand and lift the door, Acharon quietly climbed to his feet. He searched around for the crowbars, gathering them quietly. He slowly moved farther and farther away from the garage door, feeling with his feet for any obstacle that might trip him up in the dark.

From memory he was able to make his way to the door that led to the inside stairwell. He stopped to listen to the dogs. Their sounds had diminished in quantity. Perhaps some of dogs were following his scent to the car or amongst the rubble, or even back the way he'd come down Jones street, back to the monorail.

They didn't seem as intently interested in the garage door as they might if they were sure of his location, which was some relief. To be safe, however, he quietly opened the door and slipped into the stairwell that took him upstairs, turning on his flashlight only after making it to the halfway landing.

The next floor was the ground floor. There was a hallway that would lead to a window with a fire escape that would put him inside the enclave. From there it was a short distance to Pleasant Street. After that it was a zig-zag up to Huntington Park and Grace Cathedral. But just as Acharon was stepping out of the stairwell he heard music. Not from the ground floor, but from the stairwell. It was drifting down from another floor.

Might there still be someone here? Still surviving? He hadn't seen any windows lit from where he was standing outside. But he wouldn't if they were on the southwest side of the building. If they were here, why hadn't they remained in contact with Sovelet over the Internet? Whoever it was, he was sure it wasn't Thyme or his cronies. They'd have stayed to the center of the enclave, the Pacific-Union club.

Drawn by curiosity and the desire to see a friendly face, Acharon stepped back into the stairwell and started up. He stopped at the second floor and listened. The music wasn't on this floor. A quick glance down the hallway didn't reveal any light leaking under a door.

He continued upward. The music was not coming from the third floor, but as he reached the fourth floor he knew this was it. A bubbling of optimism painted a small smile on his face. He knew this floor; they'd had friends here. He followed the sound, moving in a familiar direction. The volume of the music increased as he moved closer to the door. How many hours had he spent here? He put his hand to the door and could feel the vibrations of the music. Memories of friendship and laughter echoed within the music. Late nights of card games and friendly conversation.

Could someone really still be here? And not just someone, but a friend? Could Sovelet have been mistaken after all these years?

He hoped and fought hope as he knocked on the door. "Hello?"

The music continued unchanged. Acharon put his ear to the door, listening for approaching footsteps. Hearing none, he banged on the door and shouted his inquiry once again. "Hello!?"

After no response on his second effort he gingerly tried the doorknob. The knob turned and the door swung open with some small effort. The sound of the music increased.

"Hello!? Anyone? Carter? Hillary? It's Acharon. Hello?"

Alternately watching over his shoulder and looking forward, he crept forward with baby steps, the muzzle of the shotgun pointing the way. He was in an entryway that had several closed doors to the left and right. The music came from straight ahead, the living room, so he continued in that direction. Slowly the living area exposed itself to him.

The living room was neat and organized as always. It was also covered with dust, which did not bode well. There was an entertainment center, the source of the music, a coffee table and several end tables, a couch, and two easy chairs that held two desiccated corpses. The faces were too shriveled to identify, but Acharon was sure who it was.

Carter and Hillary had lived here from the beginning of the enclave. They'd never taken the opportunity to move to the more automated condos on the other side of Huntington Park. They'd been good people. Caring people. Even now they were holding hands.

"Carter," Acharon said with a nod to the sweater-vest-wearing body. The other was in a flower-patterned blouse and white slacks. He nodded to the other and said, "Hillary."

Turning away from his old friends, Acharon stepped over to the entertainment center and turned off the power. The radio had been set to the only station that existed, playing music a hundred years old. He'd never been to the station but he knew of it, sct up to provide a source of entertainment as long as it could keep running. The small group of engineers and computer programmers who put it together said that it would probably play for several hundred years. Perhaps it would be a greeting to alien visitors. It had obviously served as an accompaniment to two deaths.

He looked around and finally saw the empty wine bottle, the two wine glasses with a hint of mold and decay in them, and an empty medicine bottle. The bottle label indicated that it had once held sleeping pills. The date on it showed the pills had been printed nineteen years ago. Had they been printed for this very purpose and used on the day they were made? Or where they an old prescription that was put to a final use?

Acharon looked around but couldn't see any sign of a suicide note. But then again, why bother? If you were one of the last people on the planet and didn't expect to be found, unlike Murphy who knew they'd be checking in on him, why waste the time writing an exclamation?

The new silence began to push against Acharon, making the room more like a tomb than a living room. He no longer wanted to be here. He left the bodies to their peace and stepped back out of the apartment. He was shutting the door with the intention of heading back to the first floor and the exit when he heard something.

It was just a small sound, a cough, a bump, something not exactly right. Acharon played the beam of the flashlight along the hallway. Go back in the apartment? That'd be a dead end. He needed an out.

Keeping an eye on the stairs down the hall, he backed up to the hall window and took a quick peek. He saw what he'd hoped to see. The fire escape was accessible from here.

He leaned his shotgun against the sill. The flashlight went on the ground, throwing a cone of light back down the hall. With both hands, Acharon pulled up on the window. It moved grudgingly a couple of inches and then jammed.

"Shit." He cursed between gritted teeth and pulled the window down and then pulled back up.

The window came up a foot and stuck again. Acharon took a moment to scan the hallway. He wasn't seeing anything, but he wasn't interested in taking chances. He pushed the window down. It fell with a slam and he quickly yanked up on the frame. The window slid up enough for Acharon to shove his pack through and then slip through himself, grabbing his shotgun and flashlight once he was on the other side.

The beam of the flashlight reflected back two glowing orbs rushing toward him. A mountain lion was sprinting toward the window. Acharon grabbed the window frame and yanked. The window slammed shut just as the cat reached him. It slammed into the window and its frame, cracking the window. It hissed at him from the other side, its teeth long and pointy.

Acharon scrambled for the ladder and hurried down, missing several rungs, scraping his shins, and banging his right elbow. He fumbled the flashlight several times, nearly dropping it as he looked up frequently. The fear that the big cat might attempt to crash through the fractured glass chased him down the ladder and onto the official grounds of the enclave.

Even when he reached the ground he continued to watch the fire escape, swinging the spot of the flashlight, stumbling over his own heels. When the shivers in his spine eased he turned and hurried down the overgrown passageway toward Pleasant Street. He took frequent glimpses over his shoulder with the flashlight, scanning every window as he went.

How or why had a mountain lion gotten into the building? Acharon knew they were in the city. They'd been seen in the parks years before he and Sovelet had left. With an absence of humans, the big cats had become curious and more adventuresome. He'd seen three of them. One he'd seen trotting down Market Street as he'd glided by on the monorail a few months before leaving the city. Until now, he'd never had a close encounter with a mountain lion before this. He'd be okay if it never happened again.

Pleasant Street was a tunnel of pitch-black darkness under a decades-old arbor. The flashlight highlighted leaves and branches with stark shadows as Acharon swung it left and right. He walked briskly down the middle of the road, occasionally catching a toe on some bit of debris hiding in the darkness.

The walk was like a time tunnel, carrying him backwards in time. There'd been streetlights here, poking their illumination between the branches, creating a lacework of light on the road. He and Sovelet had walked here hundreds of times, either on their way to dinner with friends or coming home after a lengthy dinner party. They'd be walking together, her arm wrapped around his.

That memory hurt. Acharon picked up his pace, almost trotting by the time he got to the bottom of Pleasant and turned up Taylor. Taylor still had some star-sprinkled sky peeking through the central gap between the trees. It was half a block and he was at the top.

He stopped to catch his breath and look around. Grace Cathedral to his right, Huntington Park to his left. Everything was overgrown and darker than the night sky. It hadn't always been overgrown. Even when Thyme's governance became oppressive, people made the effort to trim trees and bushes, mow the grass with the push mower. The enclave residents had taken pride in maintaining the park and the side streets. However, they weren't here any longer and nature had reasserted her dominance.

Next to the Cathedral the old Diocese building and part of the boys' school had been converted into the enclave's medical center. The front was basic care, where a person could get medicines printed and access the basic level medi-pods for minor stitches, dental, and the life-extending injections. The higher ability medi-pods were accessed through a glass hallway that connected to the converted boys' school.

Acharon trotted up the stairs to the old wood door that was the entrance to the Diocese. The inside had been converted to an open space with several medi-pods far to the left and right. He held little hope that they would be there but he checked the backs of each pod for their bio-cartridges. Unsurprisingly, there were none.

Though he doubted there would be any different situation in the medi-pods in the back, he couldn't walk away without verifying. No, he told himself, he wasn't avoiding the inevitable. Besides, Thyme shouldn't even be alive.

He moved through the building and pushed his way through the several sets of doors until he reached the glass hallway that connected the Diocese with the former boys' school. He stopped at the door. A tree had fallen. It could have happened any time in the last decade or two. The framework of the hall had stopped the tree from completely blocking his way across, but all the glass had been shattered and branches stabbed downwards into the hall. He had to stoop and then weave his way through the branches, careful not to slip on the dirt and moldering leaves.

The nurses' station on the other side was a mess. Debris and leaves had been blown around, collecting in corners and decaying slowly. There was evidence of scavenger activity around the desk. Something had clawed frantically at several of the drawers, leaving numerous scratches. Fortunately the doors to the medi-pods themselves were still latched shut. Now, if only luck would turn in his favor.

It didn't. All of the cartridges were gone.

Acharon vented his anger with a volume of swearing and by kicking an already overturned trash can in the nurses station. There was no logical reason to confiscate all the bio-cartridges. No reason unless you were already a bit crazy.

There'd been a note at the medi-fac but not here. Still, it didn't take much mental effort to put two and two together. This had to be Thyme's doing, him and his cronies. Which meant that they were most likely being stored in the Pacific-Union Club. There was no choice. Acharon would have to go there.

He used the side emergency exit that put him between the medi-pod center and the Cathedral. He hurried past where the old labyrinth had been, lost under a riot of weeds and grass. He trotted down the stairs and hurried over to California Street. There would be no shortcut through the park with its tangle of bushes and trees.

Even in the darkness the monorail track dominated the center of California Street, a gray swath across the building fronts on the other side of California. The carriage station, like a fist around the monorail, was opposite the park. The single light Acharon had seen illuminating the gate from behind was a single square of LEDs up on the platform. It seemed odd to Acharon that there were no carriages at the station. More of Thyme's doing, most likely.

Acharon turned his attention from the station back to the Pacific-Union building. With his flashlight beam leading, he hurried along the overgrown sidewalk. He was parallel with the shrub-suffocated steps leading up into Huntington park, focused on his goal, when he heard a noise.

He stopped and turned his flashlight toward the park. The bushes devoured the light, hiding anything beyond them. There were lots of small noises, almost unnoticeable noises. But this had been bigger. Too many leaves rustling, or something.

"Squirrels, maybe," Acharon said. "Big ones." He'd spoken softly, so as not to attract the attention of the squirrels.

Though he waited in silence for several more minutes, he heard nothing else. Maybe an old branch had gotten tired of fighting gravity. Maybe a bird had hopped to a new branch and missed the landing. Maybe he'd move into the center of California Street, just to be safe.

He moved more cautiously, trying to walk, not trip on debris, and listen for anything unusual in the park. The effort slowed his progress but he finally made it to the steps of the Pacific-Union building.

With renewed enthusiasm he mounted the stairs of the old club, two at a time. At the top he stopped to settle himself. It wouldn't do him any good to go around slamming things or getting mad. He needed to be focused so that he could get the cartridges and then get back to Sovelet. He turned at the thought to look at the gate blocking the monorail. Even though it was dark he could see the scaffolding on this side. It reached the roadway below. It was likely that he could open the gates from this side and walk the monorail track, accessing the carriage he'd arrived in. That would certainly speed things up.

With that settled he turned back to the door and grabbed the knob.

He expected it to be locked, but it turned as he twisted it. As he pushed the door open he heard something behind him. More annoyed than frightened, he turned just in time to see a mountain lion leaping at him. Acharon threw up his left arm in an instinctively defensive posture. The big cat crashed into him and they both fell through the doorway.

The cat had Acharon's forearm in its mouth, the teeth tearing into his skin. Acharon cried out in pain as they fell. An ear-ringing explosion of sound came from the right. The cat flew sideways, tearing Acharon's arm even more.

Acharon pushed himself further into the entryway. He held his forearm close to his chest, gripping it with his other hand. Blood seeped between his fingers. He looked about wildly, trying to determine where the cat was and what had caused the explosion of sound. His ears rang from the noise and his arm pulsed with pain.

When his head bumped against a wall he stopped moving backwards. He pushed himself up to a sitting position, arm still cradled, blood still dribbling off his good hand, and began to decipher the scene.

The cat was against the door. A large chunk of his mid-section and spine were shredded. Blood and tissue was splattered across the door. A wire lay limp on the floor, slightly pulled in the direction that Acharon had moved after the attack. One end of the wire was tied to an eyebolt in the floor past the door and the other end led to a thick metal stand on which two shotguns had been bolted. The wire ran through several pulleys and then to the triggers. It was a booby trap, one that Acharon might have fallen victim to as he rushed headlong through the doorway. As it was, falling on the wire had been enough to trigger the booby trap and inadvertently save his life. Thyme would have been disappointed with the results.

Gingerly Acharon checked his arm. There were some deep punctures and several areas where his flesh was torn. He fumbled his way out of his pack and used his right hand to find the emergency kit. In the kit were several packets of a hemostatic compound that he poured onto his wounds. Once the bleeding stopped he wrapped his arm, shirt and all, with a bandage to protect the wounds from accidentally being torn further. Just as soon as he found the bio-cartridges he would worry about his wounds.

He climbed to his feet with much hissing of breath and swearing. Once he was sure he wasn't going to pass out from pain, he began to search for more light. It would be easier to search without the burden of the flashlight.

There had been many changes to the Union-Pacific since the idea for the enclave began. Changes that would surely have the old members of the club rolling in their graves. As originally intended, the building was still a social gathering place. The difference was that anyone was now allowed through the front door.

An automatic kitchen took up the back half of the right side of the ground floor. That side was now a self-serve kitchen. The left side had been turned into a single lounge with plenty of seats, several automated mini-bars, televisions, and computer terminals.

The first floor was much the same. There was a room with game tables, pool tables, more computer terminals. toward the back of the first floor were smaller, more intimate rooms for smaller groups to meet. They'd been Thyme's favorite place to plan his rule over the enclave.

The second floor had been made over into a series of studio apartments originally intended for out-of-town visitors. Around the time Acharon had left with a bloody compress over his eye, Thyme and his goons had moved in permanently. Not that many people cared, since most had stopped making use of the facility after Thyme's treatment of the Oakland refugees.

The renovations included more accessible lighting. Acharon scanned the walls with his flashlight until it spotlighted a light switch panel with four toggles. Things were supposed to work even after long periods of dormancy. That presumed Thyme hadn't cut the wires or something along those lines.

Acharon used the flashlight for leverage and pushed the light switch up. Early dawn filled the room behind him. He flicked the next three and noon arrived inside the lounge. The flashlight, now unnecessary, was switched off and he set it on a chair nearby. Looking at the room, he could only shake his head in wonder. Whoever had been here in the last years obviously had given up caring about their environment.

The lounge was a mess. Trash littered the corners and was shoved into the unused fireplaces. Food containers were stacked and strewn, drink glasses had heads of mold topping opaque liquids or lay broken on the ground. Several large paintings from the club's history were in tatters from what Acharon took to be shotgun blasts. The further he went into the room, the worse it smelled.

He tried not to care. He was here for something specific and he wasn't planning on coming back. Still, to see one of the last homes of humanity so fouled, it was saddening. He turned around and went to the dining area past the dead mountain lion and shotgun boobytrap.

The mess continued. Tables were overturned or stacked with trays that someone was too lazy to feed into the reclaimer. Chairs were toppled or broken. The kitchen was a mold and debris haven and drove Acharon back with its smell. He was relieved not to see any of the bio-cartridges here. He'd have a difficult time trusting them to save Sovelet.

Sovelet. Time was ticking. Acharon took the stairs to the first floor at a pace better suited to an old man. The thought made him smile. Yes, he was old. Older than anyone had planned. Except for the lack of sleep and the damaged left arm, he felt a third of his biological age.

Before he found a light switch, he found a body. Its face, shriveled with time, gnawed on by hungry rodents, was unidentifiable. The clothes provided no clue to who it had been. The wide rust stain of long dried blood around the body gave some explanation as to how the person had died. Above them was a light switch, so that was some good luck.

Flicking the switch revealed more of the same disdain for neatness he'd found in the rooms below. And another body.

This one was sprawled face down with a narrow shotgun impact site on their back. Whoever had shot them had been pretty close.

Acharon looked around the mess and carnage. No weapons. Someone had come along after. No one had answered when he called out; perhaps they were dead. Or hiding. With nervous caution, he took a peek around the nearest corner to the second body. There was a dry blood trail that dribbled its way down the hall and two more bodies seemingly unconnected to it.

One of the bodies Acharon recognized as a crony of Thyme's. Both in the hallway might have been. They still had weapons close at hand or in their possession.

The blood trail led to a door and under it. Acharon tried the knob but the door was locked. If the person who had left the blood trail was still in there, and judging by how long the bodies behind him had been dead, it was probable that the one beyond the door was also dead. Still, he knocked.

"Anyone?" He asked and bent his head closer to the door.

When he received no response, Acharon pressed the barrel of the shotgun against the frame near the top hinge and pulled the trigger. The echo in the hallway was almost as shattering as the boobytrap at the front door. Worse, the recoil vibrated through his body, aggravating the wound on his left forearm. He paused to breathe through the pain and then shot the bottom hinge.

The door teetered but didn't fall. There were three hinges. Acharon checked the shotgun. Two rounds left in the tube cartridge. He chambered the next round and shot out the middle hinge.

Slowly, the door wobbled on its bottom corners and then slowly tilted into the room. As it fell a chain lock and a bolt lock were torn from the doorway frame, the wood groaning in protest.

Acharon chambered the last round for the shotgun and slowly moved onto the threshold. It was a busy room, crowded with boxes, barrels, and slumping stacks. The bio-cartridges were here. So was Thyme.

11

It was a larger room than originally intended. The scars of hasty expansion revealed where walls had been torn out to create a unified space. All the aggressively won space was lost because of the stacks and piles of supplies. Several narrow towers of boxes rose high enough to touch the high ceilings. Apparently no one involved in the bull-in-a-china-shop renovation had been an engineer or architect. The ceiling near the back of the room had partially collapsed.

The room was filled with everything. A lot of it useful, some absolutely necessary, had been hoarded in the room. And in the middle of it all, at the end of the dried blood trail, was a throne-sized chair. Slumped and shriveled, Thyme's body hung over one arm of the chair like a casually tossed rag.

There was no doubt it was Thyme. The face was indistinguishable because of the years and the decay, but the clothes were the clue. The blue jacket with the gold shoulder boards and buttons, pale with a coating of dust, held the body in a loose hug. Thyme had taken to wearing it as he exerted his authority more and more over the enclave. The jacket marked him clearly.

Thyme was the last person Acharon wanted to see. But he was as dead as anyone else Acharon had discovered since he'd returned to the enclave. Of course he expected that Thyme was dead. While Acharon would never wish someone was dead, he wasn't saddened by the discovery.

He expected everyone to be dead. It was looking as though he was right in that assumption. It was just a shame that some had to die so violently.

He walked over to the club chair. There was a dark stain on the back of the blue jacket, about where Thyme's heart would have been. Cached around Thyme's feet were two shotguns, a Winchester model 70, and eight handguns. Acharon assumed some had been confiscated from the two bodies by the stairs. The rest either belonged to Thyme or were brought here to him. What kind of paranoia had driven him to hoard essential goods and arm himself so heavily?

Whatever reason it was, Acharon doubted that it was started by someone else. And clearly whoever they were had taken an even greater dislike to Thyme than Acharon. Acharon could never have brought himself to kill someone, even if that someone had stabbed him in the eye. But he could understand how someone else might have been driven to it.

Death was the result of it all and there was nothing Acharon could do about it. He certainly wasn't going to haul all the bodies down to the rendering pod. Let them become part of the archeological mystery that humanity might one day be. For Acharon there were more important things to do.

Acharon went to the stacks of cartridges and sloughed off his pack. Despite the pain he worked with both hands. He favored his left and occasionally had to stop and let the pain subside and wipe the blood off the back of his hand. He shoved three bio-cartridges into the back. It was all that he needed and he now knew where more were. Using rope, he tied the top ends together so they wouldn't loll about in the pack like drunk soldiers, making movement awkward.

He strapped three more to the back of the pack and the crowbars to the bottom. It'd be a heavy load but he wouldn't have to carry it far. He hadn't started out with the crowbars, but they'd come in handy once already; who knew, they might be useful again.

Before leaving the room, Acharon did a quick search through the room and found fifty-five-gallon drums with men's clothes sealed inside. He worked the seal loose and popped the lid off. A burst of pain and stars in his vision forced him to pause. He breathed deep for several minutes before turning his attention back to the barrel. Inside he found jeans and shirts. Everything was a little too big for him, but he had a belt, so that wasn't a huge hurdle to overcome. He grabbed a set of clothes and carried them back to his pack.

He pulled his pack on, stumbling with the awkward weight of the cartridges. The left strap brushed his forearm and stars of pain flashed across his vision, stealing strength from his knees. The arm needed care. He picked up the clothes, staggered to his feet, and left the room without sparing a last look for Thyme.

On the ground floor he passed the dead mountain lion and tottered down the stairs to the street. He kept having to stop and wait for a wave of pain and dizziness to pass. He'd looped the clothes through the shoulder strap of the backpack to free his right hand. He carried the shotgun with effort. He'd tried to keep it up, ready in case another mountain lion decided to have a go at him, but he could barely keep the barrel from scraping against the ground.

He held the flashlight in his left hand, pointing down, illuminating barely more than the few steps in front of his feet.

As he walked, he scanned both sides of the street, the monorail, and the bushes on the edge of Huntington Park. He didn't really believe there was another mountain lion. But in his state, even an angry bunny rabbit was a threat.

Fortunately, as he took the corner and crossed Taylor Street, the only wildlife heard was small and deep in the bushes. They would be a problem only if he dropped dead. But by then he wouldn't care.

Despite himself, the thought made him shudder. He couldn't die here, not now. Sovelet lay in a medical coma while the machines breathed for her and waited for the bio-cartridges so they could print the new lungs. If he died, she would, too, and she wouldn't even know why.

The fear was like a boost of adrenaline and it carried him to the other side of Taylor and into the med-center. Inside, he locked the door and again sloughed off the pack. He dragged it to the furthest medi-pod, leaving it by the touchscreen terminal. He removed the bio-cartridges from the bottom of the pack and carried them into the back of the pod.

Pushing the cartridges into the slots was made difficult by the exhaustion weighing him down and the blood on his left hand. Twice he'd dropped the first cartridge. It was only after taking a pause to breathe and remind himself that rushing wasn't helping that he finally got all three cartridges inserted. He didn't bother with the cover, leaving it where he'd dropped it. He did shut and secure the access door. No need to give luck an ulcer.

Around the front he pushed buttons on the medi-pod terminal and the door lifted. Acharon blew a lip-popping breath of relief that shuddered into a sob of pain. He staggered inside and sat on the treatment table. With his good hand, he used the inside terminal to enter all his information that the pod's computers needed to look for his medical records.

Finally, the screen blinked ready and indicated that he was to lie back on the table. Acharon did so willingly. He lay with his eyes open and watched as the scanner moved overhead, taking vital signs and mapping his body's systems. Several spidery arms moved outward from the wall near his head. Two came with needle phalanges that moved down to his arm. He didn't watch but he could feel the needles poke his skin. Just as quickly, all the pain went away. He sighed with the sudden end to the discomfort. As he closed his eyes in relief he saw several more arms moving to his left side.

He'd been completely unconscious when the pod at the medi-fac had removed the damaged eyeball and replaced it with a newly printed eye. There'd been only the most minor discomfort when he'd woken. At the beginning of his life, such technology was in its infancy, and pain management was still an iffy science. He'd always wondered if all of humanity had applied its combined abilities long before the Last Wave was born; could they have thwarted the sterilization of humankind? Why did it take the end of the species to finally bring them all together?

These were the kinds of thing that Acharon often mused on when he was sitting alone or lying awake in the middle of the night, watching Sovelet sleep. There'd been very little violence when he was born and he'd grown up in a world where most of humanity was collaborating to make its last citizens' farewell a comfortable one.

A digital bell dinged. Acharon opened his eyes. All of the pod's arms were gone, retracted back into the main body. He sat up and looked at the screen. He'd fallen asleep for three and a half hours. It was just after five in the morning. If he hadn't seen the time on the screen's clock when he'd entered, he'd have thought he'd been asleep for an entire evening, which would have been a heart-rending situation.

As for his arm, it had four deep lacerations that had been sealed and covered with synthetic skin. The other punctures and tears had been superficial and needed only cleaning and a fresh bandage. The pod's screen had left a message informing him that it had analyzed his state of exhaustion and had given him an energy-boosting supplement. That would explain the refreshed feeling.

Acharon jumped off the table with a little more of his normal spring. His arm didn't hurt, he had energy. He felt more confident than he had in hours. He was going to make it back. Sovelet was going to be okay. They'd go back home soon enough and get back to living their quiet lives.

With his renewed energy, he quickly stripped off his ripped, torn, and blood stained clothes. The pants felt uncomfortably wide in the waist and he had to ease off a belt hole to keep them from pinching his skin.

Dressed in fresh, clean clothes, he snatched up his backpack, slinging it across his shoulders, and grabbed the shotgun and the flashlight. Outside he took a moment to look around. The sky was dark to the west but paling to the east with a hint of orange. He no longer needed the flashlight to find his way through the dark to reach the monorail. He took up a light jog down the stairs and then up Tayor. In a few minutes he was on California Street and nearing Thyme's wall.

It was only an assumption on Acharon's part, but he was pretty sure that the scaffolding set up on both sides of the monorail track were meant to serve as guard towers. Had Thyme forgotten that there were very few people left in the world? Certainly not enough to build an army and come attack his little fiefdom on the hill. But the towers' presence, in consideration of the gate across the track, was useful to Acharon. It was going to make his exit easier. He hoped.

At the scaffolding he took a few seconds to push the flashlight into the pack. He slung the shotgun over his shoulders, letting it rest across the pack.

He began to monkey his way up the scaffolding. He pulled with his arms, pushed with his legs, and jumped where necessary. He could have moved slowly, more cautiously, but the renewal of energy was too enticing and he couldn't help a little playfulness. Imagine a hundred-year-old person at the end of the twentieth century moving so easily.

At the top of the scaffolding he crossed over to the monorail track. Examining the three crossbars more closely, he laughed with relief and energy. They merely hung across uprights of thick metal welded to the gates. Acharon lifted up the first one and threw it aside. He watched it clatter and clang down the scaffolding like a mad bell. The other two followed quickly behind.

The gate was slightly more complicated. It hadn't been assembled with long-term usage in mind. The hinges were rusted and he wasn't able to get his fingers around an edge to pull. He had to take off his pack to free a crowbar.

That was exactly what he needed. With a little leverage the right door squeaked open enough for him to grab and put his back into the effort. He pulled until he had enough space to slip through. Once through, he pulled the pack after and secured the crowbar before sliding the pack straps over his shoulders.

The carriage was still where Acharon had left it. He would have been surprised if it hadn't been. As he walked along the rail he heard sounds below him. They were clicking sounds. Then there were whimpering sounds. He moved close to the edge and looked down.

"Well, crap."

A pack of dogs was moving just below him. Acharon was still pretty sure they weren't the same pack that had pursued them to the medi-fac, but he wouldn't bet anything valuable. They followed him as he continued toward the pod. They bounced and jumped with an eager energy, the teeth glistening with drool. When he used the rail of the carriage to scoot around to the door the dogs began barking in excitement. He wondered if they were hoping to spook him, causing him to lose his grip. If that was the plan, it failed as he slipped inside the carriage.

He set the pack on the floor of the carriage and began working at the panel. He got the doors to close and then overrode the destination program and sent the carriage sliding back to the medi-fac where Sovelet waited without knowing.

Below him he watched the dogs racing after the carriage. They continued for several blocks before they slowed to a trot and then stopped the pursuit altogether. Several of them scratched at themselves and then the whole pack set off in a direction north of California Street.

Acharon moved to what was now the front of the carriage and watched the monorail track rush under. Far away, the ocean was beginning to reveal itself with the fading of night.

The carriage worked its way around and through the switch area and then rushed up the hill toward the medi-fac. Acharon shielded his eyes against the morning sun and watched the track closely as the carriage approached the building. He watched the courtyard where he'd driven the Jeep in less than twelve hours ago. He leaned as far to the right as he could, forehead pressed against the glass windshield. There was still a glow of lights from inside the wall. If only the track ran closer to the front of the building or the wall around the ambulance entrance had been lower.

The carriage slowed on its approach as the doors on the second floor slid open like arms opening for a hug. For the briefest of moments he had a view into the yard. Just as quickly it was gone. But in that brief moment it looked as if he'd seen something move.

The carriage slid into the station as quietly as it had left. Acharon watched the station platform for movement as the carriage slowed and came to a stop inches from the next one. He hadn't seen anything but he quickly grabbed up the pack and took the safety off the shotgun, holding it ready to defend himself if need be.

The doors opened silently. Acharon waited. There were no sounds of hunting dogs, no sound of nails clicking on the tiles. No snuffling, no baying. Acharon leaned forward, peeking out beyond the doors of the carriage. He saw nothing and slowly moved forward, the barrel of the shotgun leading the way.

He stepped out of the carriage and stopped to listen again. Once more, he heard nothing and slowly moved further and further away from the carriage until he was committed to the goal of the elevator.

Acharon stopped at the elevator, his finger just about to touch the call button. He wasn't concerned that the dogs had gotten on the elevator. He was sure that it was still waiting, just beyond the closed doors. He did wonder if they'd only gotten into the garage or if they'd made it all the way into the building. He needed to know.

He walked away from the elevator and pushed open the door to the stairwell. Standing just inside the stairwell, his hand holding the door ajar, he listened for any sounds that might alert him to the dogs. He heard nothing and stepped in. He only had to go down one floor. He took the half-flight to where the stairs turned back on themselves and checked the first floor door. It was shut. He hurried down to it and braced himself against it, pressing an ear to it. He listened for several minutes and heard absolutely nothing except his own heavy breathing.

He turned and peeked through the little window in the door. The room looked exactly as he'd last seen it. There was a little more light now because of the wind turbines. It was more than enough light to see the chair he'd wedged under the door handle to the garage.

Acharon pulled the stairwell door open and led with the shotgun as he stepped into the waiting room. He moved on tiptoes, crossing to the door and chair wedged under its handle. He slowly looked out through the window.

He found himself staring at a dog. It was sitting on the hood of the Jeep. It was the big dog, the one he thought of as the leader of the pack that had made their trip to the medi-fac so miserable.

It looked right back at Acharon.

Acharon moved and so did the dog. It barked as it ran and jumped. Its forepaws struck the door with enough energy to make the door quiver. Other dogs joined in with the barking, sending up a cacophony of noise that sent Acharon backing toward the stairwell. When the door handle jerked down against the chair, he ran.

He ran up the stairs to the second floor and pushed the call button. The elevator doors opened and he rushed in, pushing the floor five button and then the doors-closed button repeatedly until the doors did close and he heard the grind of the gears driving the elevator up.

By the time the doors opened on the fifth floor Acharon had calmed down. He'd wiped the sweat of fear from his forehead on his shirt sleeve. He had no problem admitting that the dogs had scared him and he was glad to be many floors above them. He'd worry about how they were going to get out of the hospital after Sovelet recovered.

Back in room three, Sovelet looked no different than when Acharon had left. It made him feel more positive about her chances.

It took only a few minutes to load the bio-cartridges in the back of the medi-pod. Around front he flipped through the control panels until he found the one to make the pod's computers check the cartridges. There was a brief pause and an image of the bio-cartridge schematic popped up on the screen. The images of the cartridges were red. After a few more seconds they slowly faded to green. Acharon heard the whirring of gears and the hush of pistons moving. He stepped back and saw the arms beginning to move. Elsewhere in the machine he could hear thumps and grinds as the organ printer began its job of making new lungs for Sovelet.

Acharon stepped back from the pod. Now it was a matter of waiting. And while he waited, maybe he could get past his fear of the dogs and devise a plan to get around them.

12

"I miss anything?"

Acharon jumped when he heard Sovelet's voice. He'd been lost in his thoughts and hadn't realized she'd finally woken.

"Hey, you're awake," he said. He went to her bedside and kissed her on the cheek, lingering. "I thought you'd sleep a bit longer."

They were in one of the small recovery rooms. The automated bed had moved when it was time, carrying Sovelet from the medi-pod and down the hall. The beds did a transfer by themselves, sliding Sovelet over. The room matched her temperature, as did the recovery bed. Previously, a nurse would have stopped by to pull a sheet over the patient. Acharon had done that for Sovelet before settling in a chair. He'd been watching her breath and his mind had drifted off to problems past and present.

Now Sovelet was awake and pointing at his left arm. "What happened?" she asked.

Acharon sat on the edge of the bed and told her everything that had happened. While he didn't spare any of the details, he may have under-exaggerated them. Sovelet stared wide-eyed through the entire story.

"I can't leave you alone at all."

Acharon laughed. "I'm sorry. I didn't try to get into trouble."

"It's okay," she said and patted his right hand. "I know you wouldn't do something so foolish on purpose."

He squeezed her hand with his left and they lapsed into a moment of comfortable silence. They'd both been through a lot in the last two days. It seemed, though, that there was still a lot more to go through.

"So now what do we do about the dogs downstairs?" Her question echoed his own thoughts.

He got up and walked to the window. He pushed a curtain aside and looked out on a sun-bright sky. There were a few clouds drifting over the city. Several turkey vultures glided in wide circles. Shadows from the buildings were long slashes across the cityscape.

"It's too late to try and get back to the warehouse. If we have problems, even a flat tire, working in the dark will be difficult."

"And the dogs."

"Yes," Acharon said. "The dogs, too. I don't think they go home after an eight-hour shift. And it'd be hard to see them at night."

"And if we wait until daylight, we'll still have to deal with the dogs."

"They might leave." Even though he said it, he didn't feel it.

"They might not."

Acharon nodded in agreement. "You're right. They've been determined and patient so far. I don't know if they'll give up at all. They're curious."

"They want to kill us."

Acharon recalled the alpha dog jumping at him from the other side of the door. It elevated his heart rate just remembering. "Well, I don't think they want to be friends."

"So, what are we going to do?"

"Rest some more. Sleep," Acharon said. He smiled at the look Sovelet gave him. She didn't like being an invalid, even a recovering one. "In the morning, if the dogs are still there, we'll need to lure them away from the Jeep. I think there's a way to trap them in the building. But not until the morning, when you're ready."

"I'm ready now." Her brow furrowed and Acharon knew she was going to ask something. "Why aren't we taking one of the carriages? You took one to the enclave. Why not just keep going?"

He'd thought about that, too.

"We don't know if there's any more damage to the rail," he said. He knew Sovelet could check the system online and probably would. "And even if we got all the way back to the Embarcadero terminal, we still have to get to the warehouse. We'd have to walk the distance."

"And the dogs." Sovelet nodded.

"The dogs," echoed Acharon. "And while I'd like nothing more than to be sitting on our island with a cup of hot tea, it's still better to wait. It'll be dark soon. We're better off waiting until morning. So, until then, we need to rest. Then we'll do what we have to do to get home."

"And where are you going to sleep?"

He opened a cabinet that served as a window seat. Inside, sealed inside thick plastic bags were pillows and blankets. "The chair I was sitting in reclines to a twin bed."

"They're not very comfortable," Sovelet said. She had the experience from their last visit to call upon.

"It'll be fine."

They talked more about Acharon's trip to the enclave. Sovelet questioned him over details until she realized she was hungry. Acharon was glad to fetch food from the cafeteria. It gave him a break from retelling the story of the evening's adventure. What happened sounded exciting in the retelling, but the violence of the mountain lion and Thyme's death still bothered him.

The cafeteria made some pie and chamomile tea for dessert. The tea did its job and Sovelet became sleepy. He finally persuaded her to sleep and tucked her in with a kiss. After dimming the lights and pulling off his boots and socks, Acharon lay down on the chair, now serving duty as a twin bed. As he settled in, pulling a sheet over himself, he looked up to see her watching him.

"Get some sleep," he said.

"You too." She closed her eyes.

Acharon relaxed as best he could. He shifted several times in the first few minutes, his body as restless as his mind. As he shifted for a fourth time, he began to mull over escape plans. Some of them were elaborate, requiring a hot air balloon and favorable winds. Others were disastrous, ending in their being mauled to death by the dogs. This continued until his mind drifted off of its own volition and he dreamed.

In his sleep he was chased by dogs through an apartment building. He was always escaping but they were always finding him. Doors that should have led to a stairwell led back to the hallway. Places where doors should have been didn't have doors. The dogs came through the windows and doorways. The halls filled with dogs. There was a tidal wave of dogs.

Acharon groaned and rolled over and all the dogs disappeared, the dreams went away, and he slept deeply.

When he did wake, it was to the sound of plastic clicking. At first he thought it was another dream. Dog claws tapping across the floor. Then he placed the sound. He was listening to a keyboard. He rolled over to see that Sovelet was no longer on the recovery bed. He angled his head toward the only terminal in the room.

Sovelet was sitting on a stool, the heels of her shoes hooked in the lower cross bar. Her hair hung loose and looked as though she'd been brushing it not long ago. She was bent forward over the keyboard, her focus on the screen where all Acharon could see was lines of code.

"I miss anything?"

Sovelet screamed and stumbled off the stool.

"You trying to give an old lady a heart attack?"

Acharon sat up and pulled on his socks.

"You're not an old lady," he said. He found his boots and pulled them on.

"I'm a hundred and forty-five. I'm an old woman. You're an old man."

She'd returned to the computer terminal and in a few keystrokes she cleared the screen.

"I felt like one yesterday," Acharon said. "I don't feel like one now. And you don't look like an old lady."

"Thank you, that's very sweet. Don't scare me again."

Acharon saluted. "Yes, ma'am. What were you working on?"

"The usual," she said. Then, "So you have a plan, yes? For the dogs."

"I do. I think. Only one way to find out. You ready?"

"I was ready hours ago."

A side benefit of the rapid advances in medicines and life-sustaining biology was the rapid recovery time from any surgery. Acharon had been up in mere hours after a full eye replacement. A day was more than enough for surgery requiring the opening of a human chest.

He stood and stretched. A glance at the curtained window, which glowed with daylight, indicated that they were already well into the morning.

"Let's see if the auto-mat still has coffee. Maybe something filling to eat." He knew it was stalling, but he was really hungry and it seemed smarter to deal with the dogs on a full stomach rather than a distracting empty one.

The auto-mat, as it turned out, still had coffee, and pancakes with syrup. They both had seconds and then sat for a few minutes in their normal, companionable silence. Shortly, he thought he could feel the pressure of Sovelet watching him. Waiting.

"And now I'm ready to deal with the dogs," Acharon said. He stood and held out a hand for Sovelet.

Dealing with the dogs required rope. A lot of rope. More rope than Acharon had. They improvised by tearing bed sheets and tying the pieces together.

"They don't have to be strong enough to hold anyone," he told Sovelet. "We just need it to last for ten, fifteen minutes."

When they had the two hundred feet of combined sheet and rope, Acharon carried it to the stairwell. He started on the third floor, letting out the rope as he went down the stairs to the first floor. Along the way he ran the rope over and around the stairwell railing. He smeared synthetic petroleum jelly wherever the rope would come in contact with the rail. When he reached the first floor, a quick peek through the door window showed that the chair blocking the garage door was still in place.

He moved slowly to the chair, keeping low enough not to be seen by any of the dogs that might be present. With the last of the rope he wove a pattern through the chair and up to the handle. Tugging on the rope would cause the chair to fall and pull the door handle down at the same time.

Testing the rope attracted the attention of a single dog. It barked repeatedly but never attacked the door. Its volume faded. Curious, Acharon hazarded a look through the window. He was ready for the alpha dog to jump at the window but he was absent. The barking dog had gone out of the garage into the courtyard still blanketed in the long shadows of morning. It continued to bark, its whole body coming off the ground with each vocalization.

Acharon had a moment's urge to open the door and race to the button that would bring the gate down. It would take maybe a minute to untie and move the chair. They'd have easy access to the Jeep. But then what?

Before he could commit to the idea, though, he heard a growing chorus of dogs barking. In moments the courtyard and then the area around the Jeep was a chaos of barking and jumping dogs. It seemed that the first dog's barking had been a call to duty. He and Sovelet would be sticking to the original plan.

He searched around for a trash can and set it so that when the door opened it would fall into the gap. This would hopefully keep the door open after he pulled away the chair and the dogs pushed past the opening door.

When he was sure everything was set the way he'd planned it, he began a retreat to the stairwell that was hastened by the sound of several dogs slamming against the door.

Acharon looked over his shoulder as he hurried to the stairwell door and tripped over the rope he'd laid out. The line between his foot and the chair went taut. He could see the chair move an inch, maybe two. The dogs continued to attack the door. The handle wobbled with their activity, but the chair continued to hold.

With the extra incentive to hurry, Acharon carefully freed his foot and jogged up the stairs to the third floor, mindful of the rope and sheet line that wound its way upward with him.

He exited at the third floor. Sovelet was there, working at a nurses' station terminal.

"That doesn't look like security cameras to me."

Sovelet switched views to another program window that showed images from six closed circuit cameras. They showed the garage, the first floor waiting room, and the second floor stairwell landing.

"That's because I was already done with them." She pointed to the image from the garage. "Look."

Acharon bent closer to see what she was pointing at. The garage was filled with more than a dozen dogs. Some continued to bark and jump at the door. Others milled about sniffing each other and everything else. A few, like the Alpha sat with their heads cocked as if listening.

"I saw the one dog and was going to suggest closing the gate."

"My thought, too," Acharon said.

"But then there were dogs everywhere. And look."

Sovelet clicked on the monitor window for the courtyard. It expanded to fill the screen. Sitting just inside the entrance was the alpha dog. There was no mistaking its look. It was the same dog, still.

"He's been there since you left the lobby," Sovelet said.

Acharon shivered at the thought.

"You think this will work?" Sovelet asked. "Will he fall for the trick?

"It's what I got. I think it'll work. One way to find out." He squeezed Sovelet's shoulder. "You ready?"

Sovelet held up her two-way radio. "Ready."

She gave him a good-luck kiss and he headed back to the first floor.

For Acharon, this was the scary part. He had to get the dogs' attention. He needed them riled up and eager for the chase because they all had to come after him or it wasn't going to work.

When he reached the door to the garage he gave his contraption one last look. Everything seemed in order.

"One, two, three," he said into the radio.

"Ready, set, go," Sovelet responded.

Acharon stepped to the window and rapped on it with his knuckles.

"Here, kitty kitty," he said.

His taunt wasn't needed. Before his knuckles had touched the glass a second time, the dogs were up and barking, jumping at the door window. Acharon could hear the snap of the jaws as they bit empty air. He had to resist the urge to flee. He banged on the door a few more times.

The door handle rattled vigorously. It was time.

He ran back to the stairwell and up to the second floor landing.

"Here we go," he said into the radio.

He pocketed the radio and grabbed the sheet rope and pulled slowly and firmly. He didn't want to yank the rope in case it knocked things the wrong way or knocked them loose when they shouldn't. He heard the sound of the chair falling and then the clang of the trashcan falling, hopefully blocking the door open.

"They're in," Sovelet said over the radio.

Even without her warning, Acharon knew they were in the building. They sent up a cacophony of barks that was near deafening. He released the rope and dashed up to the third floor.

"They've found the stairs," Sovelet said as Acharon rounded the half-flight to the third floor.

The rope kept the first floor door to the stairwell open. The barking got louder as the dogs entered the stairwell, following Acharon's scent. He was through the third floor door and was pulling it shut as the first dogs were between the second and third floor landings. Their speed surprised him and he almost didn't get the door shut in time. He looped a waiting line of real rope around the door handle. The other end was secured to a door handle near the nurse's station.

The dogs arrived, barking and jumping. To get in, they would have to pull the door open. It was something he didn't believe they could do. But he'd also believed they couldn't get the gate to the garage open.

"How we doing?" he asked.

"It looks like they're all out of the garage," Sovelet said. "Still a few in the waiting area. The rest are on the stairs. I didn't think there were so many of them."

"What about the alpha dog?" Acharon asked. He risked a peek through the stairwell door. The activity on the other side escalated.

"I saw him move after the other dogs charged the open door. I can't see him now." She paused. Acharon could imagine her scanning the monitor feeds. "I don't see him. He's probably in the stairwell."

Acharon wasn't going to risk another look. "Well, let me know when they're all in the stairwell."

He reached down and grabbed the sheet rope just past where it ran in from under the stairwell door. He sat and braced his feet against the doorjamb on either side.

"A couple more," Sovelet said. Acharon could hear the tension in her voice. "Almost."

Acharon slowly pulled on the sheet rope, taking up slack and hopefully not attracting any attention from the dogs. The sound beyond the door was like sharp-pitched thunder. Acharon stopped pulling on the rope when he felt tension in the line. Now he waited.

"Get ready," Sovelet said after several long minutes.

Acharon was surprised the dogs were still trying to bark their way through the door.

"Now now now," Sovelet said. She'd jumped up and knocked over the stool she'd been sitting on.

Acharon yanked on the sheet rope. There was a moment of tension and then it came loose. He pulled furiously, drawing the rope under the door, piling it between his legs. Several times the rope went tight and began to slide back under the door. He was caught in a tug of war with one of the dogs on the other side of the door. Behind him he could hear Sovelet righting her stool.

"The door on the first floor is shut."

Acharon cut the real rope from the rest made with sheets and scrambled to his feet. He started coiling the rope as he moved over to the monitor where Sovelet was righting the stool.

"Well?" Acharon asked. He scanned the images from the cameras, seeking his own answer.

"I think they're all there," Sovelet said.

"Think they are?"

Sovelet pointed at the waiting room camera screen. "I thought I saw movement, but I was busy falling off my stool.

"Are you okay?"

"Bruised my pride."

"You'll recover." He gave her a hug and a kiss. "We'll wait a few minutes and see if there's any movement."

They watched the screen together. Acharon stared hard enough that his eyes would ache and he'd have to blink several times. Together they watched for ten minutes. Occasionally, Acharon would scan the other camera images. The dogs in the stairwell had finally worked out that they were trapped. They barked on occasion and jumped at the door. Many of them were sitting or curled up on the landings.

"I must have been wrong," Sovelet said after a few more minutes.

Acharon gave the waiting room screen a few more seconds of his attention.

"All right. We'll go. We'll just be cautious."

Sovelet shut down the computer programs she'd been running. Acharon strapped the rope to the backpack before he hefted it onto his shoulders. He gave the shotgun one last check, making sure he'd loaded the cartridge cylinder. When Sovelet looked at him and nodded he led the way past the stairwell door. The dogs, sensing their approach, began barking furiously. Acharon could see the tops of their heads through the window as they jumped in front of the door in frustration.

At the elevator he tapped the call button.

"So I'll exit first, just to be safe. Stay close. Let me know if you see anything."

"Yes, sir." It was said with a salute and a raspberry.

"Insubordination."

The elevator dinged and the doors slid open. Acharon stepped halfway through and waved Sovelet in.

As the elevator ground its way to the first floor, Acharon flexed his hands on the shotgun. The first two shells were buckshot. He wasn't taking chances. He was playing for keeps. The dogs gave every clue that they weren't playing around and so neither was Acharon. He was sure that right now Sovelet wouldn't begrudge him his intentions to protect them even at the cost of a dog's life.

The elevator dinged for the first floor. Acharon looked at Sovelet and nodded. She nodded in return and stepped backwards to be behind him.

The doors slid open. Acharon stepped forward, pressing his left foot against the door to keep it from shutting. The barrel of the shotgun panned across the waiting room. When he failed to see any movement he moved into the room. He could feel Sovelet moving behind him, the weight of her hand on the backpack. They walked toward the garage door. Acharon kept scanning with the shotgun as they neared the door. The trash can was still jammed between the door and its frame.

"Ach," Sovelet said. Her hand touched his shoulder. He could feel it shaking.

Acharon spun around to face in the direction Sovelet was looking.

The alpha dog was standing on the far side of the reception counter. Its hackles were raised and a low growl was slowly rising to an audible level across the room. It began to pace slowly toward them, teeth bared.

"Anything behind us?" Acharon asked.

There was a pause during which the Alpha had moved two steps closer.

"If you mean any other dogs, then no. Nothing."

"Move to the door, open it wide enough for us both to get through," Acharon said.

Sovelet moved toward the door. The alpha dog hunched, looking as if it planned to leap. Acharon brought the shotgun's barrel up, pointing directly at the Alpha's face. The dog stopped. Its growl deeper, louder. Acharon could feel a cold shiver wriggle up his spine.

There was noise of metal scraping the ground behind Acharon. "I'm here."

Acharon nodded and backed toward the door. The Alpha matched his movements, step for step. It switched from growls to barks. Loud barks that flicked spittle onto the floor and into the air. Acharon's finger began to apply pressure to the trigger. He knew he should kill the dog. Kill it now and be done with it. He'd had to do it before. It was self-defense. Self-defense was justified.

He should do it, but did he have a right? It wasn't the dog's fault he and Sovelet were here, looking like a threat. When had mankind ever not looked like a threat. As much as the dog scared him, he didn't want to do it. Not if they could both just walk away from this. Soon enough the city would be his and Acharon would be on his island. May they never meet again.

Acharon stepped backwards over the threshold of the door. His mind was still a riot of emotions and thoughts. On the side of his vision he could see Sovelet's hand pressed against the door, keeping it open. The dog was still maintaining its distance.

"Let it go," he said. He sounded as if he'd just come back from the dentist, his words having to push past the stock of the shotgun pressed against his cheek.

Sovelet's hand disappeared from view and the door started to swing shut. The Alpha dog waited until Acharon started to lower the shotgun and then lunged at the door. Acharon grabbed the handle and pulled the door shut. Rather than closing completely, the door stopped closing and slowly jerked the other way.

"Ach!"

Acharon passed Sovelet the shotgun and grabbed the door handle with both hands. He could feel movement in the handle. The dog had grabbed it on the other side, shaking it like a caught rabbit. Acharon yanked on the handle once, twice, and the door slammed into the frame. The latch clicked as it caught the face plate. Acharon backed away.

"That was close."

"It's not over," Sovelet said.

Acharon looked at the door. The door handle was no longer jiggling. Rather, it was moving slowly up and down, like someone testing a door to see if it was locked.

"We should go," Acharon said. He helped Sovelet into the Jeep. As he ran around to his side he kept an eye on the door handle. The handle turned downward with more force. He was pretty sure that the dog was going to get the door open any second.

Acharon backed the Jeep out of the garage and set the brake.

"What are you doing?"

"Shutting the garage gate."

Acharon ran to the garage entrance and smacked the red button. The mechanism growled and the door began to slowly come down to close off the entrance. He ran back to the Jeep and jumped in.

"You know that he can just open that thing."

"I know." Acharon was looking over his shoulder as he turned the jeep around. "But at least this'll slow him down."

Acharon pulled out onto Parnassus and turned left.

"You didn't shoot him, either," Sovelet said. "I really thought you were."

"I should have. I know. I just couldn't squeeze the trigger. I don't want to hurt anything, Sovie, I just want to go home. I want them to ignore us."

"We've lost our position on the top of the food chain," Sovelet said.

"By default."

Sovelet laughed. "Yes, by default. But now we're the hunted and not the hunter."

"I doubt the deer and the pigs have shotguns."

Sovelet shifted in her seat to look at him more fully, though her eyes drifted to the road behind them. "What's that supposed to mean?"

"Deer and pigs evade the predators. They run away, they hide, they outrun. They don't pull out a shotgun."

"Because they can't. We can. Some animals have the natural ability to defend themselves. Even early man would have made a spear and used a rock."

"You hear yourself," Acharon said. He was grinning. "You're advocating the killing of animals. After all these years."

"Yeah, because they're trying to kill us."

"Well, it doesn't matter. We're out of there and will be at the warehouse in an hour, hour and a half. Then it'll all be behind us."

Sovelet looked out the back of the Jeep. "I hope so."

13

"We turned left," Sovelet said. She'd sat quietly for several blocks. She'd then turned left and right in her seat, attempting to orient herself. "Is that right? We turned left?"

"Wasn't sure if the dogs escaped that they wouldn't head back the way we came here," Acharon said.

He slowed the Jeep and turned right onto 3rd Avenue.

"You're trying to shake them?"

"I'm not sure we can shake them if they catch us again. I was just hoping to confuse them, at least for a bit."

"They're trapped in the medi-fac."

Acharon slowed as they bumped and rocked along 3rd Avenue, which was in terrible shape. With fifty-plus years to themselves, the trees had pushed up the old asphalt near the sidewalks. They created hillocks of petroleum-based stone covered with grass and native flowers.

"You saw that dog yanking on the handle," Acharon said. He slowed a little more as the Jeep rolled up and over a particularly rough patch of earth-buried road. "It might only be a matter of time."

"I thought I was the cautious one."

"You are. I'm the paranoid one."

After the ragged passage down 3rd, Acharon drove across Lincoln Way and onto Kezar Drive. Kezar Drive was a meandering road that cut across the southeast corner of Golden Gate Park, paralleling and then slipping under the monorail, and dumped traffic out onto Fell Street. Rather than continuing on to Fell, Acharon turned left on Stanyan Street.

"What way are we taking back to the waterfront?"

"Geary to Kearny to Broadway."

"That seems a bit convoluted," said Sovelet.

"I agree. I also agree that I don't want to deal with that dog and its pack. Thank you."

They fell silent again as the Jeep worked its way up the sloop of Stanyan toward Fulton. As they crested the rise and began the long slope down to Geary, a thought occurred to Acharon.

"Now that I think about it," he said, "I hope the dogs do get out."

"Really? Why would you wish such a thing?"

"We might need to go back again sometime. It's the best facility, the most options."

"You also said the pods at the enclave are still good, too," Sovelet said. "You know where all the bio-cartridges are located. And it'd be safer. Despite the mountain lion, which isn't nearly as common as dogs. Besides."

"'Besides'? Besides what?"

Sovelet was quiet for a fraction of a minute. She looked out at the passing buildings. "We might not ever come back."

Acharon chewed on her words for a few minutes. He gave half his attention to the Jeep as he turned it around the short curves just before the right onto Geary. What did she mean, he wondered. Was she going to refuse any more invasive help from the medi-pods? Was she giving up?

"Are you giving up?" He repeated his thought out loud.

"No, Ach. That's not what I'm saying."

They turned right onto Geary. The street was wide, lined with thick, towering trees, the median a riot of overgrown bushes and weeds. Several deer bolted as they saw the Jeep come onto the street.

"What are you saying?"

The whole purpose of the final, concentrated efforts of those who preceded the Last Wavers was to ensure they could live long, healthy lives. To extend the presence of humanity as far into the future as they could. There had been plenty of Last Wavers who had rejected the idea of an extended life. For a brief time there'd even been suicide cults which had decimated the Last Wave population. Even Sovelet had been shocked by their actions.

All of them confused Acharon. He'd tried to understand their position, but he couldn't accept it. Why end your life prematurely? Perhaps they were afraid they'd be the last one left on the planet. Maybe they just couldn't imagine living into their mid-one hundreds. But the second protocol of all life is to live. Reproduce first, if you have the ability to do so, then live your life. Not throw it away.

"I'm not saying what you're thinking. I'm not lying down. I'm just saying things can change."

Acharon saw her wrap herself in her arms. Her knees squeezed together and pointed away from him. Fourteen decades keeping each other company, he knew those signals. He pressed his lips together to keep words from accidentally slipping out and focused on the drive down Geary.

Since he was putting more attention on where he was going rather than trying to coax conversation from Sovelet, he saw the problem with the Masonic underpass before they were close.

"Detour," Acharon said. He took a right at Wood Street.

Sovelet looked past Acharon at the Masonic Avenue underpass.

"It just collapsed?"

"Not just, I'm sure. But it's not exactly an area that got a lot of attention." Acharon turned left onto Anza Street, which would become O'Farrell Street in a few blocks. "Not every building got the plastic coating, very few roads got maintenance bots. And how long had that bridge been there? Two hundred fifty years? Longer?"

"It's just shocking, I guess." She threw her hands up in the air. "I know, I know, we've seen collapse everywhere, but when you haven't seen something in a while and then suddenly you see it and it's not as you remember, well, it's shocking."

Acharon nodded. Sometimes even seeing the same change many times was shocking. When the center span of the Golden Gate Bridge had collapsed he was stunned and awed. For weeks after, wherever he happened to be, if he caught a glimpse of the space where the bridge had been, the same feelings emerged again.

He turned the Jeep left onto Divisadero Street and a minute later a right turn put them back on Geary.

"Ach, isn't there a station coming up in Japantown?"

Stations were outposts for the slowly shrinking population. Rather than travel all the way to the enclave or medi-fac for a check-up or first aid, people could stop in at one of the stations. There were a dozen of them spread out through the city. Once most of the Last Wavers had taken up residence in the enclave they became more like rest stops. If a person or group was out in the city, sightseeing or merely nosing around, the stations became places where people could find food, sleep, recharge a car, or pick up a new one. It was almost like a roadside rest stop but self-contained.

"Yes. Why?"

"Don't laugh, but I have to use the bathroom."

Acharon didn't laugh, but he did smile.

The access to the outpost was through the old underground parking garage. Entrance was off Post Street. Acharon turned down Webster and then left.

"Look out!"

Acharon hit the brakes on the Jeep. It skidded on the debris-covered road. The jeep slowly spun as they slid past a brown bear. Acharon shifted the Jeep into reverse and stepped on the pedal. The engine whined as it fought to provide the energy that Acharon needed.

The bear had also been surprised by the sudden appearance of the Jeep. It had lumbered down Post in the opposite direction for twenty feet before stopping and looking back at the Jeep. It then began to lumber back toward them, twisting its head and roaring at them.

"At least it's not dogs?"

Acharon was holding onto the back of Sovelet's seat while he steered the Jeep in the backward direction. "Dogs can't tear the roof of this car like a pull tab on an olive can."

"Oh, that's right," Sovelet said. Now she looked nervous. "Can we outrun it?"

"Probably." Acharon shifted back to forward. "But we just have to outmaneuver it. Not the sharpest turners." He applied enough pressure to the brake to stop the Jeep quickly but not so much that it spun again. He put his foot back on the accelerator and they rolled back the way they'd come.

Acharon raced the Jeep toward Webster Street. The bear continued to charge toward them. As the Jeep drew closer to a collision with the bear, Acharon jammed the brake pedal to the floorboards and put left pressure on the steering wheel. The Jeep slid and started to spin counterclockwise. The bear rushed past, slipping and falling off its back feet in the process.

Acharon stepped on the accelerator again and the Jeep rushed forward on its new trajectory. As the Jeep picked up speed Acharon began rolling down his window.

"You're going to shoot the bear?"

"You know I can't," Acharon said. He pointed to the garage entrance. "I'm going to get us inside."

"Why don't we just keep going?"

Acharon checked the rearview mirror. The bear was loping in their direction but didn't seem as if it was charging after them.

"You said you had to pee."

"I can hold it."

Acharon laughed. Despite the danger, their banter never failed to lift his spirits.

"Well, apparently the Jeep can't. The charge on the batteries is low. Too low."

He stopped the Jeep in front of a roll-down gate and reached out to a panel. He flipped up a cover and pressed a button.

"Let me know when we have room," he said. He twisted in the seat to keep an eye on the bear. He could hear the gears reluctantly coming back to life, yanking the gate free of decades of debris. The bear had slowed. Perhaps it was suspicious of the Jeep just standing still. Deer would have kept running. And the sound of the gate probably didn't help.

"It's up."

Acharon stepped on the accelerator enough to roll the Jeep into the garage. Just inside was another pedestal with another panel and covered button. He pushed the button. The gate rolled down, faster than when it went up. The bear had stopped, staying back from the gate as it clanked into place, blocking the entrance. It sniffed around and then meandered across the center divider of Post and into a stand of trees and undergrowth.

Acharon drove the Jeep over to a series of charging stations.

"I thought you said we had enough charge to get to the medi-fac and back."

"I did say that," Acharon said. He'd climbed out of the Jeep and was unhooking the charging cable. "I said that because that was supposed to be true. So either the car has a problem or the batteries do or we somehow used more energy than we realized. And you wanted to go to the bathroom."

Acharon pointed to a set of double doors.

Beyond the doors was a series of rooms for all necessities of human comfort. They could relieve themselves, pick up some new clothes if desired, check email, get stitches or a check-up, and hopefully get a cup of coffee.

Sovelet went on ahead and Acharon turned his attention to the Jeep. He checked connections to the batteries. He'd put them in so he wasn't surprised to find the connections still firm. He hadn't hooked the Jeep to a charger at the medi-fac, but he'd believed the Jeep's charge would hold. So that left the batteries themselves. No plan is ever perfect and it was likely that one or more of the batteries were defective.

He got the Jeep connected to the charging station. The readout said an hour to top off the batteries. Even a full, defective battery should get them back to the warehouse if it got them this far in the first place. Time to find a cup of coffee.

The inside of the station was much like a hotel lobby, minus the desk to check in and out. There were couches and chairs for resting in. Along one wall was a series of automated vending machines. To the left was the door to the medi-pod and basic supplies. Beyond a door on the right was a hallway that led to private rooms where a person or persons could stay the night if they didn't want to travel the city in the dark or just needed to get away. And a person didn't have to lose an eye to stay here.

Sovelet wasn't in sight. Acharon presumed she'd made a beeline to one of the wash closets. He turned his attention to one of the coffee machines and was gratified to see the machine beep and blink to life and make a cup of coffee. He watched with some amusement and nostalgia as he listened to the whirring and clunking and gurgling. Soon enough, the little door slid up and a cup of coffee was gently pushed forward. The steam drifted lazily upward, twisting violently when Acharon picked up the cup and walked over to a couch to wait.

He and Sovelet had made use of similar stations in the city and the one on Treasure Island. They became respites from the escalating drama of the politics at the enclave. That was when the wall around the enclave started going up. That was when Acharon realized what Thyme was really trying to do. Perhaps he could have adapted and learned to live with the self-anointed leader of the enclave, but it was the addition of the Oakland enclave refugees that changed everything. Thyme's treatment of the 'outsiders' was deplorable and offensive to the other members of the enclave. But few spoke up. Then things started getting ugly. Then Acharon had stepped in. And the rest was history.

Still, the stations were a nice memory.

He looked up as the door latch clicked.

"Everything come out okay?"

"That was old a hundred and thirty years ago." She looked around and then walked over to a row of terminals.

"It's not everyone that can make that claim. Coffee?"

"Really?" She'd sat on a stool and was bringing a monitor to life. "There's still coffee?"

"If you apply the term loosely. But it's hot."

"Sure." She focused on the terminal, her fingers clicking rapidly across the keys.

Acharon looked at the terminal in passing. He saw several windows open, lines of code, a map. "What are you doing?"

"Catching up on stuff."

Acharon shrugged and made his way to the automated coffee vendor and punched up an order for two black coffees. Sovelet had been the primary force that kept the distant members of the Last Wave connected. As the number of computer specialists plummeted, she'd taken on more and more of the responsibility. The few chat rooms that still saw traffic existed because of her ability to remotely keep servers alive. When connections were lost she would dig and dig until she was able to reroute new ones. Last New Year's she'd had every remaining enclave and connected individual on line. She'd found and played for twenty-four hours, videos of fireworks and countdowns. It made him wonder what she would do when there was no one left to communicate with. What would she do when the little white dots on her world map were reduced to just one, just north of San Francisco.

"Coffee?"

"What?" He turned around. He'd been spacing out, staring a thousand yards beyond the vending machine, into the past and the future. "Right, coffee. Still hot."

He set the coffee on the counter by the terminal and Sovelet picked it up without looking, her eyes focused on the lines of code. "A few more minutes."

"All right." He went back to the couch and sat. It was actually good to sit and relax without having to worry about being mauled by bears or ravaged by dogs. It was, for the moment, like old times. His memories stayed with him until he heard the sound of a stool scraping the floor. Sovelet was on her feet, dropping her coffee cup into the recycler. The monitor she'd been working at was dark. His coffee had grown cold. Time had flown.

"I'm done," Sovelet said.

Acharon followed her. He slipped his cup through the refuse hatch. He could hear the shredder and grinder kick in. They'd reduce anything to mulch and, if the rest of the machinery were still working, it would be compressed into a compost brick that would have been picked up on a regular schedule. That was when everything was still working. Which he knew wasn't the case.

Acharon went through the doors to the garage first. He moved slowly, scanning the parking area for any creature that might be a threat. He was pretty much of the opinion that if there'd been a rabbit he would have treated it with the same wariness as the bear.

At the car he held the door open for Sovelet. When she was safely inside the car he unplugged the charger and got into the car. He turned the key to check the battery charge.

"We have enough juice?"

"It looks like it," he said. He released the brake and backed the car out of the spot. "But that's what I said when we left the warehouse. Fortunately we're not that far away now. This misadventure is almost over."

He slipped the Jeep into drive and steered toward the gate. This time the gate slid upward with less complaining. The shadows of the trees and buildings were short and pointing east. The day was half over. At least the dogs were gone, as was the bear. His fingers were crossed against anything else going wrong.

14

They stayed on Post Street rather than work their way back to Geary. There'd been no further sign of the bear as they'd left the station. Near Van Ness they had to pause while a mother skunk and her little ones crossed in front of them. The mother skunk had paused only once as she emerged from a tangle of grass and weeds to their left. After watching the Jeep for several moments it seemed she'd found it not to be a threat. With the little ones scurrying after her, the mother skunk waddled across the road and up the dirt-sloped curb on the other side. As quickly as they'd appeared, they disappeared into a small copse of saplings.

Acharon saw the wistful smile form on Sovelet's lips as she watched the babies trundling along after their mother.

There were other signs of wildlife as they continued. Raccoons and squirrels, birds, all of them seemed to be in abundance amongst the trees. Trees that had cracked their way through sidewalks, seemingly determined to push aside all that humanity had built.

The going was peaceful. Acharon and Sovelet easily shifted into the kind of small talk that would fill the hours on their island. As the decaying buildings and towering trees rolled past, they talked of the vegetables in the garden and whether they needed another layer of compost before next summer.

It took a while, but it slowly occurred to Acharon that he was doing most of the talking, doing most of the planning. Sovelet had often been the first to suggest increasing rows of beans or adding more tomatoes. Yet now she was nodding and agreeing with him in a distracted voice. Her tone was that of someone not really interested in what was being discussed.

"Sovie? Is everything okay?" He gave her a quick look before looking ahead again. They'd just passed Union Square and it was only a couple more blocks to Montgomery Street. It was a left turn after that and then on to Broadway.

"Yes. Everything's fine."

"I don't mean to nag." Acharon paused. The quiet of the electric motor in the Jeep meant that he could hear birds singing in the trees, the tires crunching over the ragged street. Other sounds. "Do you hear a rumbling?"

"Thunder?" She leaned sideways to look up at the sky.

"No, a rumble. I can't figure it out." He slowed the Jeep and rolled the window down completely. "You hear it?"

"Earthquake." Her suggestion was half-hearted. The sound wasn't coming from below. They weren't feeling it.

"No, I don't think so."

Sovelet rolled down her window. She listened, with her head cocked, her ear angled upwards. "Yes. I hear it. It's echoing off the buildings. Could there be another vehicle?"

"What vehicle makes that noise?" Acharon was twisting in his seat as he looked left and right and over his shoulder. It wasn't barking that he was hearing, but it still made him nervous.

"Careful!"

Acharon yanked on the wheel. He'd been heading toward a vine-covered bus stop. "Sorry."

"Just be careful." She stuck her head out of the window, pulling herself closer to the door with both hands. "I think it's getting closer. It's definitely getting louder."

"But from where?" He pushed down on the pedal. There couldn't be anyone else alive in the city. It couldn't be a street cleaner unless its software had somehow gotten buggy and restarted itself. Sovelet would say that wasn't possible. So he didn't entertain the thought for more than a second. He just wanted to get back to the warehouse and get out of the city.

"Louder."

"I hear it, too." He lifted his foot off the accelerator. Were they running into whatever it was? Should he turn down another street or turn around?

"Ach." Her voice was peaked with fear. "Go faster."

Acharon looked into the rearview mirror. He pushed the accelerator to the floorboard. The Jeep's wheels spun uselessly before they tore up enough moss and dirt to grab the exposed asphalt and shove the Jeep forward.

Behind them, white eyed and thundering toward them, was a herd of Elk.

"Do something, Ach, I think they're getting closer."

The Jeep shot past Grant Street. Acharon mentally cursed himself for the miss. He'd intended turning at Grant. Now they'd have to try turning on Kearny, going full speed before the elk caught up to them. A quick peek in the rearview mirror showed them quickly closing the distance.

"Hang on, Sovie. Left turn, coming up."

"Crap, Acharon. Can you slow down?" She turned to face front and tried to cinch her seatbelt tighter.

Acharon took a peek in the rearview mirror. The elk were less than a block behind the Jeep.

"We're going to have to chance it."

He steered the Jeep to the right side of the road, hoping for a wider angle. As the elk thundered closer he pulled the steering wheel counter-clockwise and the Jeep turned sharply toward Kearny. Acharon was sweating and his heart was thumping wildly but he was certain they were going to make the corner.

There was a thump against the back of the Jeep and the rearend bucked. Acharon caught a glimpse of an elk with a rack of horn stumble and then regain its footing. But the Jeep was already sliding sideways.

Sovelet screamed.

The Jeep continued to slide and then it began to tilt, coming off its left wheels. It crashed onto its side. Acharon held the steering wheel as his body was jerked to the right. The seatbelt dug deep into his right hip and left shoulder.

Sovelet was still screaming. Her hands were pressed against the frame of the door and roof, keeping her from touching the ground sliding by her opened window.

With another crash the Jeep came to an abrupt stop. Acharon's hands were torn from the steering wheel and he slipped further down toward Sovelet, the seatbelt barely holding him to the edge of his seat.

Outside the Jeep the thunder of stampeding hooves was fading.

"Sovie? Sovelet?"

"I'm okay," she said. Her voice cracked with fear and ended with a sob. He could see her moving.

"Are you sure?" He needed her to be okay. They were a long way from any kind of medical help.

"Yes. Just shook up. Definitely going to have some bruises. What about you?"

"My shoulder hurts," he said. He was trying to find a way to brace himself so that he could undo his seatbelt without dropping on her. "I must have wrenched it when the Jeep hit the building."

The building was directly in front of them. The hood and the front of the roof were crushed against stone and steel. The windshield was a concave spiderweb.

Acharon finally got his feet braced and wrestled with the seatbelt. It took several curse-backed efforts before it clicked loose. He stepped on the ground outside Sovelet's door and freed her from her seatbelt as well.

"Nothing's broken?" he asked.

"Doesn't feel like it. Limbs all work and I'm breathing okay."

"Good. Me, too. I think." He pointed to his backpack and duffel bag. "Can you reach those?"

Sovelet looked behind her and nodded. She bent at the knees and felt behind the back of her seat until her fingers touched straps.

As she handed Acharon the pack and duffel bag he pushed them out his open window where they tipped over the side and thumped heavily against the ground. He then gave Sovelet a hand and a shove to get her up and out the same window. She slid to the side as he clambered out with the shotgun in tow.

Acharon jumped down and gave Sovelet an assist.

"That was scary," he said.

"Do you really think they would have run over us?"

Acharon checked his bags for damage and missing gear. "They ran into us. The real question is what made them stampede. Maybe it was that bear. Or another mountain lion."

"No, it wasn't."

"You seem pretty sure." Acharon stood as he slipped into the backpack straps.

"Very sure. Ach." She was pointing with a single finger, barely raised, as if to avoid detection.

Acharon turned around. A half a block back up Post several dogs were trotting toward them. Their tongues lolled out the sides of their mouths and their rib cages expanded and contracted, wide and rapid. They'd been running. They were also led by the Alpha Acharon had trapped in the medi-fac.

"Shit," Acharon said. "This way."

He directed Sovelet with a hand around her upper arm as she kept looking back.

"Am I crazy?" she asked. "Did those dogs cause the elk to stampede? To stop us? That's crazy, right?"

"We'll be fine, Sovie," Acharon said. He was looking at the buildings, looking for doors. There was an alley. "Down here."

He wasn't sure who came up with the policy to leave all doors unlocked, but he was currently grateful for it. As the population dwindled someone decided that there wasn't any reason for unoccupied buildings to remain locked. Who would vandalize them? What did it matter about who owned the building when there was no one left? The last survivors might need access to them and they shouldn't have to break a window to get inside.

And right now, Acharon needed access. The dogs had begun barking wildly and were quickly answered by other dogs barking in response from further up on Kearny. They were being boxed in.

"It's an alley," Sovelet said. Her voice was rising in pitch and she started to slow down at the alley entrance.

"Trust me."

Acharon pushed Sovelet forward to a door in the side of the building on the left. He pulled the handle. It cooperated grudgingly, squealing in protest as Acharon fought against the decades of debris and neglect. He didn't need it to open all the way, just enough.

"In," he said as the door provided a large enough gap. His own voice betrayed his fears. He didn't have enough of any kind of ammo for the shotgun or pistol to fight off a pack of dogs as large as this one was sounding to be. Even if all he carried was ammunition, he knew he couldn't reload fast enough to stop them all.

Sovelet ran to the door, turning sideways to slip in. She caught her heel and tripped. Acharon kicked her foot, pushing it through. He tossed the duffel bag next to her, followed by the pack before stepping inside himself. He hauled on the door to close it. It swung slowly shut and then stopped several inches short of the frame. Dirt and twigs had mounded up when the door scraped open and then pushed the debris forward as the door shut.

At that moment, before he could open the door to push away the impromptu doorstop, the dogs arrived. They arrived with growls and bared teeth. Forepaws scrabbled at Acharon and noses pressed into the gap. Acharon leaned away from the dogs, unable to kick at them for fear he might lose leverage and they might paw their way through.

"My pack," he said. More dogs pressed into the gap, crawling over each other. "The rope."

He could hear Sovelet pulling on the pack. He could hear her rapid breathing. He could hear the breath of panic.

"Okay. Okay. I got it. What do I do?"

"Tie a knot." He pointed with his chin to the stair railing over his shoulder. "Tie as many as you need. Just so it doesn't slip loose. Hurry. Please."

"Knots. Lots of knots." Her footsteps, which would have echoed in the silence of an empty building, were barely audible over the barking of dogs and snapping of their jaws.

Acharon turned back to the door. He wasn't sure but it seemed the gap had widened just a fraction. The angry jaws and spittle-flecked teeth seemed closer. His ears were starting to hurt from the incessant barking. He'd never thought to carry a dog whistle and he wondered now, as he held on for their lives, if they even worked.

"Okay, now what?"

Sovelet was standing behind him, the side farthest from the angry mob of canines. She held the other end of the rope in her hands. Hands that were shaking.

"You tied a good knot?"

"Yes." She nodded her head vigorously.

"You need to loop the other end around this push bar on the door."

"The dogs," she said. Her voice was choking in her throat.

"Loop it near my hand and then slide it over. You can do it."

Sovelet slipped around his left side and threaded the rope over the push bar until it piled upon itself at the bottom of the door. She used her foot to pull the grounded rope away from the door before going back around Acharon to pick up the loose end.

"Tie it back at the rail?"

Acharon nodded. "Pull it tight."

Acharon watched the slack rope rise as Sovelet pulled on it. It stiffened to a straight line and Acharon strained against the dogs and the door to allow Sovelet to pull it even tighter. There were yelps of pain and several dog snouts quickly withdrew from the gap.

Acharon's arms ached. His left knee sparkled with pain. He wasn't sure how long he'd be able to hold the door.

"I got it," he heard Sovelet say. And then, "I hope."

He looked to the rope. It seemed tight and it was stiff rope with no stretch. Slowly he relaxed his grip. The door opened a fraction of an inch and even though it wasn't much it encouraged the dogs who again began pressing into the gap with snapping jaws.

He relaxed a little more. The door stayed. The rope remained in place. He breathed a heavy sigh of relief and then grabbed the shotgun and duffel bag.

"You're not going to shoot them?"

Acharon looked at the shotgun, then back at the dogs. The gap seemed wider. Faces were more visible. He waved Sovelet up the stairs.

"I don't know if this is the time to waste the ammo I have. As long as we can get away without having to kill them, I think we're better off."

"Think they'd get riled up?" She pushed through another door.

Acharon stepped through and pushed the door shut. He regretted the loss of the rope.

"They might take it personally," he said. "Their behavior is different than dogs when we were kids. They're more aggressive, for one."

"And more aware?"

They were in a glass fronted shop. Empty mannequins and empty shelves were lined up in neat rows, waiting a future that would never come. Acharon started for a side door that didn't open on Kearney.

"Don't they seem more aware?" Sovelet continued. "Maybe that's how wolves are. I don't know."

He wound his way around a last slew of mannequins and was two yards from the door when barking came from Kearney Street. A dozen dogs came dashing around the corner, barking at the building. He stepped back amongst the mannequins.

"Back," he said. He bumped into Sovelet who steadied him with a hand.

"Can we go up?" she asked.

"Looks like we're going to have to try."

They returned to the back hall. The dogs were still pawing and snapping through the gap. Several had worked their heads completely through. Their actions increased at the sight of Acharon and Sovelet.

"The stairs are over here," Sovelet said.

"Right behind you."

When he heard her moving up the stairs he backed to them, watching the dogs. One began to worry at the rope holding the door in place. Acharon turned and hurried after Sovelet.

"How far?"

"Third," Acharon said. He stayed behind Sovelet, resisting the urge to push her faster. "We need to get out of the stairwell. Fast."

"Again?"

"Yes."

Just at the third floor, as Sovelet was pulling the door open, Acharon heard a burst of activity. The barking increased in volume and he could hear the scrape and tick-tack of claws on the smooth surface just inside the alley exit.

He stepped through the doorway, pressing against Sovelet in his haste, and pulled the door shut just as he heard the first dog barking in the stairwell.

Sovelet was leaning against a wall, holding her side and breathing heavily. She looked up at Acharon and gave him a weak smile.

"This is beginning to become a habit with us."

"Not for long. This way."

He marched down the hall. He was looking for the windows on the back of the building. Windows that looked onto the Crocker Galleria. It had been one of the many places that people had suggested for a pre-built greenhouse. Unfortunately it got too much shade and the distance from the enclave made it a poor candidate. Fortunately, Acharon had been part of the group to survey many of the buildings that were suggested as being useful to the Last Wavers. If he could get to the roof, he could get them inside.

Noise on the other side of the stairwell door caused him to turn and look. The tops of dogs' heads popped into view in the stairwell door window and just as quickly disappeared. Several dogs scratched at the door and at least one of them had ahold of the handle and was shaking it. Pretty soon they'd all learn how to open doors and nowhere would be safe.

"Down here," Sovelet said from around a corner.

Acharon turned and trotted around the corner to join her. They were in a short hallway that ended with a solid window that wasn't designed to open. He stepped to the window and looked out. The roof of the galleria was two feet down.

"Get behind me," he said. He checked the shotgun. It was loaded with plastics and salts. "Hold this. Thank you."

Sovelet took the shotgun. Acharon unlocked the handgun holster and pulled the gun out. He pushed the safety off and shot the window three times. In the reverberating silence the dogs paused in their barking. Perhaps they heard the echo of a distant memory. Acharon went to the window and kicked out the pieces along the bottom of the frame. The dogs started again with scratching and barking.

"Ready?"

"Yes." She handed the shotgun back and stepped onto the window frame and took the short jump to the galleria roof.

Acharon took one more look down the hallway and then followed Sovelet out the window. She was already moving toward a raised metal access hatch. He crossed the roof, sidestepping to keep an eye on the gaping hole in the window. He'd been able to shut doors and slam windows shut, but there was nothing he could do to stop them from coming out onto the galleria roof. The best plan was to not be there when they arrived. Acharon no longer kidded himself with the concept of *if* they arrived.

The hatch was rusty. It hadn't received the plastic treatment once the building had been dropped from the list of viable options. It was not going to lift easily.

Acharon shed his pack and untied the crowbars secured there since the enclave. He worked his way around the edges of the hatch lid, pulling at the metal lip with the hooked end of the crowbar. He went around twice, moving quickly and on the second pass the hatch popped loose.

He lifted the lid, grateful for his gloves or he'd be needing a visit to the nearest medi-pod for an old-fashioned tetanus shot.

"Go, I'll drop you the gear."

Gingerly, Sovelet stepped onto the ladder, pressing firmly on each rung before moving all her weight onto it. Halfway down she stopped and held up a hand. Acharon passed her the duffel bag and she lowered it before dropping it the final few feet. The backpack followed. Acharon hung the shotgun over his shoulder by its sling. He was slipping into the opening when he heard the first bark at the shot-out window. He looked up to see several dogs jumping from the window and sprinting toward him.

Acharon grabbed the crowbar and flung it at the dogs. They twisted away but one was hit by the straight end of the bar, causing the dog to yelp and run back, tail between its legs. Acharon used the brief pause to pull the roof hatch closed. As he climbed down the ladder he could hear the dogs jumping on the hatch, a ragged chorus of barks and growls following.

On the ground, Acharon slipped on his pack and grabbed the

duffel bag. They were in a back hallway. They needed to find the entrance to the main part of the galleria and the walkway that crossed over to the other side.

Sovelet was staring up at the hatch that echoed with the paws of the angry dogs.

"We're going to get out of this, right?" She looked to Acharon. Worry lines criss-crossed her forehead.

"Yes," he said. He stepped over and took her hand in his. "We'll make it home. I promise."

She smiled and fell into step beside him as they looked for the door to the main hall.

Acharon smiled back. Now all he had to do was keep that promise.

15

"What is this?"

"I've never looked," Acharon said. He peeled back more of the foil from the energy bar he was chewing with all the enthusiasm of eating glue and sawdust. "I don't want to look."

"Do we have enough water to get these down?"

"No."

Sovelet handed the rest of her energy bar back to Acharon. "Then I'm done."

They were sitting on the floor on the opposite side of the galleria from where they'd entered. Overhead, they could see dogs trotting along the side of the glass half-tube that ran down the center of the roof. Occasionally one of the dogs would try to run over the top, but it was too steep, too slippery with moss and dirt, and it would inevitably slide back.

It had been Acharon's idea to stop and eat something. They'd been moving since they'd trapped the dogs back at the medi-fac. A temporary trap as it turned out. He was tired and he knew, despite her efforts to hide it, Sovelet was tired, too. They needed to rest and he needed to think. The shadows were already crossing the street and they still had a long way to go. What they needed was a vehicle. Something sturdy to get them to the warehouse. Once inside the gates they'd be safe and two steps from home. He wasn't sure when he'd want to leave the island, if ever, once he set his feet back on it.

"You need the energy," Acharon said. He picked up the energy bar and held it out for her.

Sovelet shook her head. That and the stubborn press of her lips told Acharon that he should just let it lie. There was better food if they could get to another station. But there wasn't a station going north that was close enough. They'd have to cover ten or more blocks with the dogs hounding them.

Acharon sat up, stiff with a shock of adrenaline and realization. North might not work, but east just might. He jumped to his feet and started stuffing food wrappers back into the duffel bag. He could have left them. Who would know? But he wasn't raised that way and Sovelet would chide him for leaving trash.

"You thought of something."

"I did. Two blocks east. First and Market."

Sovelet looked confused and then grinned. "A station."

"And I'm pretty sure we can get there through the buildings. We just need to shake them for a few minutes to cross the street."

Sovelet helped to pack the last of the items pulled from the duffel bag and backpack. Acharon grabbed the shotgun and then pulled the backpack straps over his shoulders. Sovelet was zipping the duffel bag shut. When she was done he reached for its handles. Sovelet grabbed them first and pulled the duffel bag closer.

"In another era I would have been an invalid for months. But I'm not. So you'll stop treating me like one. You'll let me help."

"It's been a long day," Acharon said.

"And it's not over. It's you who shouldn't wear yourself out, doing all the carrying and shooting."

Acharon nodded in acceptance. He gave her a quick kiss and then headed along the concourse, looking for the stairs down. Sovelet followed close. He heard the occasional shuffle of her feet as she turned to look over her shoulder.

They went into the sub-level and the parking garage. The parking garage was open and accessible. The dogs could already be down here. They appeared to understand the idea of cutting off their prey. Acharon wouldn't have been surprised to hear them barking as they neared the doors. However, he had no intention of entering the actual parking area. He only needed to pass through to the next building. There were service access points that allowed just that.

It took a half hour before he finally found a door that let them through to the towering building next door on the corner of Montgomery and Sutter. Up one flight of stairs and they were in the lobby. Acharon stayed to the shadows, keeping as much out of sight of the windows as he could until he was certain the dogs hadn't surrounded the entire block. Again, he wouldn't be surprised if they had.

"There," Sovelet whispered.

Acharon followed her pointing finger. A lone dog was trotting past on Montgomery and then turning on Sutter. It stopped for a moment, its nose working furiously, and then it continued down Sutter.

"Sentry," Acharon said. He shrugged, not sure if applying human concepts made sense. But animals in large groups had members who kept an eye or ear out for danger. Meerkats and gophers came to mind. "But if it's a lone sentry and we move fast, it might work."

"Where are we going?"

"Straight across Montgomery. Into the next building."

"That one?" Sovelet pointed to the tower across the street. A Starbucks sign was on the front of the building. It was sprouting weeds where the birds had left nests and guano behind. Just to the right of the sign was the building entrance.

"Exactly. Just keep moving and I'll cover for us both."

"That's a revolving door over there."

Acharon had to look again. A revolving door. Dogs could push revolving doors. He'd have to do something.

"All right," he said after some thought. "Soon as you're through, look for a chair or something and I'll hold the door if they come. We can wedge it in place."

"Maybe a couple chairs." Sovelet grinned as she said it, but there wasn't any humor to it.

"Probably a good idea. Ready?"

Once Sovelet nodded agreement, Acharon started trotting to the Montgomery Street exit of the building. He could feel the pressure of Sovelet's hand on his shoulder as she stayed close. The duffel bumped against his backside every couple of steps. They reached the door and Acharon pushed through. He scanned left and right as Sovelet came around and began to run ahead of him. He followed quickly on her heels and continued to move after as she reached the revolving door.

Sovelet pushed and the door refused to budge.

"Stuck!" Her voice was a harsh whisper.

Acharon hurried over and helped her. They pushed and pulled, trying to break loose all the debris. Like the hatch at the top of the galleria, each effort moved the door a little more and then a little more.

A dog barked. It was close by.

"Keep going," Acharon said. He turned to face the street.

A dog was across the street on the corner. It was the same one he'd seen trot by just before they ran out of the building. It was barking at them and then barking off to one side.

Other barks sounded in response.

Acharon shouldered the shotgun and took aim at the dog. He pulled the trigger and fired a round of rock salt toward the dog. He had no expectation of hurting it, but the sound sent it scrambling down Sutter.

"I'm in," Sovelet said.

Acharon looked over his shoulder to see the door slowly turning. Sovelet was halfway inside. He stepped back into the next opening of the revolving door and pushed with one hand as he watched the opposite street corner.

The barking had increased tenfold and was growing louder. Dozens of dogs came racing around the corner as Acharon's section of the door turned far enough to cut him off from the dogs. A few of the dogs made it into the next section of the revolving door. Acharon leaned against the incoming door wing to impede its momentum. His weight and decades of disuse stopped the door's motion. The dogs jumped against the glass, barking furiously.

"I got this," Sovelet said.

Acharon looked to see Sovelet dragging a large trash can. "There's more of them," she said as she dropped the first one into the gap.

"Bring as many as you can," Acharon said.

Sovelet ran off and quickly returned, dragging two more.

"Don't hurt yourself."

"Better I hurt myself than they hurt me."

Acharon wanted to laugh, but the dogs were taking all the humor out of the day. "Good point."

Two more trips and Sovelet had enough trash cans to fill the doorway and keep the doors from spinning.

Acharon stepped back to catch his breath. The dogs trapped in the door were pushing on both sides of their section, battling themselves. More dogs had arrived, pacing back and forth in front of the glass windows. One of them, however, sat and watched Acharon through the glass.

"He's still here," Acharon said.

"Who? The alpha dog?"

Acharon pointed. The Alpha growled in response.

"That dog does not like us."

Acharon nodded in agreement. "I should have shot it when I had the chance."

"But you didn't. That's water under the bridge. It's here. We're here. So what's next?"

"We need to get from here to the next building."

"That's possible?"

Acharon turned away from the building front and started walking deeper into the building.

"I'm counting on it."

A lot of creativity was involved in getting away from Montgomery Street. The block they were traversing was a wedge shape between Montgomery, Sutter, and Market. The buildings in that block were of diverse sizes. Acharon had to break a window to get out of the building. From there, most of the travel was on the rooftops. They climbed over the edges, dropping down or clambering up.

They moved through long shadows. The sun was now halfway between its zenith and the eastern horizon. They could still reach the warehouse before they lost all light. But only if he could keep them moving and find a vehicle.

Several times as they crossed building tops, he took a peek over the edge. Each time he caught a quick glimpse of several dogs down on the street. They sniffed at everything but they still seemed intent on the building Acharon and Sovelet had entered and already evacuated.

How long before the alpha dog worked out what they were doing and moved to interfere. Acharon needed it to be too late to catch them. In either case, all he could do was keep moving and look optimistic. He was pretty sure Sovelet couldn't smell fear, but she might be able to see it.

Finally, they reached the corner where Sutter and Market met. They stood far back from the glass doors looking out onto a corner courtyard. Once it had been a quiet place for financiers to make phone calls and drink fancy coffee drinks. Now it was a jungle, topped with towering palm trees. The ground in the courtyard was a hazard of pushed-up tiles, the cracks crowned with weeds.

"I can't see anything through all this," Sovelet said.

"Well, if we can't see out, they can't see in. Maybe."

"But they can smell."

Acharon had moved up to the doors. He began to experimentally push on a door. His efforts were stymied by debris and broken tiles.

"Good point," he said as he moved to another door. "Any idea which way the wind is blowing?"

"No." It was an automatic response. She was already studying the tops of the palm trees, hoping for an answer.

Acharon was trying to open a door as silently as possible. Pushing and pulling slowly, repeatedly, gently scraping away the weeds and dirt. He had no idea how far the dogs were ranging in an effort to hem Sovelet and him in. They probably heard as well as they smelled and he needed to get himself and Sovelet across the street. If they were cornered here he wasn't sure exactly what he could do next.

When he had enough of a gap to slip through he dropped the backpack outside. Sovelet handed him the duffel bag and he pushed it out next. Fortunately neither he or Sovelet had ever put on excess weight, so getting through the narrow gap wasn't too painful and only cost Acharon one button off his shirt.

Once they were both through, he pushed the door shut and jammed dirt and tile pieces against it. If the dogs were in the building or got in, they wouldn't find this exit an easy one.

"No going back now," Sovelet said.

"No going back." Acharon hefted the pack onto his shoulders as Sovelet again snatched the duffel bag before he could reach it.

Several birds flew up from the weeds and bushes as they pushed slowly through. Acharon repeatedly caught his feet against the tumbled-tile ground as he obsessively scanned in the directions of Sutter and Market. He'd pause at random, causing Sovelet to bump into the pack he carried. Her mumbled curses would have amused Acharon if he'd actually been paying attention to them.

When they finally reached the ivy-choked columns that marked the boundary of the courtyard, Acharon edged forward. He used the chaotic ivy as camouflage. Left and right there was only the silent buildings and the flora that was slowly breaking the city down. There were no animals, except the few birds he could hear singing in the branches. No sign of raccoons or skunks, or even turkeys. More importantly, there wasn't any sign of the dogs, not even a distant bark -- which might have been something to worry about.

There was another park across Bush. It was bordered with towering weeds. Spindly trees dotted the area. A building had been there once but had been torn down as part of the early Earth Reclamation Movement. The building had been removed, the concrete and bricks pulled up and native plants put in. The other native plants, otherwise known as weeds, proved to be heartier for city life and they overpowered the more innocuous foliage.

"We have to cross to there," Acharon said. "Then we have to pass through there. Almost to our destination."

Sovelet hefted the duffel bag up with both hands. "Then let's go."

Acharon nodded and led the way across the street and through the weed fence. A few rabbits dodged into holes and birds flitted off to more distant limbs. The world remained quiet, at peace or in anticipation, depending on the level of paranoia a person was feeling. Acharon was feeling paranoid.

It all went back to the one dog, the one he and Sovelet called the alpha dog. Wherever they found themselves harassed by the growing pack, the alpha was present. He didn't appear to be opportunistic, he appeared to be in charge. And he appeared to be clever. So to think that they had outsmarted Alpha and his pack, well, Acharon would wait until he was safe on the island before he believed it.

Then, as if the dogs were only waiting for him to feel the smallest bit of confidence, he heard barking. Fortunately, the sound was behind them.

"We need to move a little faster."

Sovelet answered by moving more rapidly, requiring Acharon to take several jogging steps to catch up.

Then they heard dogs somewhere out in front of them.

"They circled us?" Sovelet asked. She'd stopped and was turning in one spot, as if she might be able to locate them with some sense other than hearing and sight.

"Encircled, I imagine."

"Herding us." Sovelet shivered.

Acharon understood. The skin over his spine had felt like something was crawling on it. They'd been tricked by the dogs into thinking they were safe. The dogs had remained silent, probably aware of Acharon's and Sovelet's presence the entire time. Now, out in the open with no building instantly accessible, the dogs were making their move. They were going to drive the two humans in a direction advantageous for them. Acharon needed to find a way to make it work for them instead.

"And there," Sovelet said. She was pointing toward Market Street. "More of them."

Acharon listened. The dogs were on Bush, Market, and ahead of them on Battery. They needed to get past Battery and there they'd find the station. The dogs, however, wanted them to go elsewhere. Acharon knew where he'd like the dogs to go.

"Left. That's where they're trying to force us." He looked left and then up toward a building. That was exactly the kind of place they could find some refuge. Why push them in that direction?

Acharon moved tentatively toward the building, more than twenty floors and weathered. The window glass, like on so many other buildings, were streaked with decades of collected dust washed by the occasional rains. The barking behind them got louder.

"They're coming closer." Sovelet bumped into him as she kept twisting to look over her shoulder.

"That's just to encourage us to keep moving," Acharon said. He pushed through the last of the weeds and saw why this was a good direction to be shoved by the dogs. The building rested on squared pillars. The first floor was more open space than enclosed foyer, wrapped in glass. There was one section, the middle of the Market Street side, that was a concrete column stuck to the side of the building, running up the side of the building to the roof. If they got caught trying to run around it, there'd be no shelter.

The building was also isolated from other buildings. So even once inside, they'd have nowhere to go. But it was better than no place at all.

"Run," he said and pulled Sovelet along.

They rushed toward the glass box that was a small portion of the building's actual footprint. Several dogs came sprinting across the open from the left and the right. Acharon pulled on Sovelet, jerking her forward.

"The duffel bag!"

"Keep moving!" Acharon stepped back and hefted the duffel bag over a shoulder. He could see dogs moving slowly through the undergrowth he and Sovelet had already left behind. Two dogs had trotted out ahead of the others, teeth bared in a drool-dripping growl.

Acharon pointed the shotgun in their general direction and pulled the trigger. The sound shocked all the dogs and the rubber pellets sent the two he'd aimed toward running and yelping in the opposite direction. He turned and sprinted after Sovelet.

He passed her just as they stepped onto the buckled concrete skirt of the building. He yanked on the door before him. It didn't budge. He pushed and it slid open with some effort. Doors that could be pushed open from the outside. Never a good situation. Once he pulled Sovelet through, he dumped the duffel bag and pack and pulled the second crowbar from the bottom of the pack, and wedged it through the door handles. As he did, he noticed the locks. Simple paddles to slip the latch.

A quick look around revealed doors in the other glass walls. He set the locks and then ran without explaining, twisting the latch on the second set of doors. Sovelet saw what he was doing and ran in the other direction. Acharon raced to the third set of doors and locked them. He looked up and lunged backwards as two of the largest dogs slammed into the doors. The doors shook with the impact but held.

"Ach!"

Sovelet's scream of his name roused Acharon. He jumped up and hurried toward the last set of doors. Sovelet was struggling with one of the doors, trying to push it closed while several dogs pushed back. As he drew closer, Acharon could see the reason for fear in Sovelet's voice. One of the dogs had pushed its head through the gap. Its jaws were clamped onto Sovelet's jacket sleeve. The dog was shaking Sovelet's arm as if it had a cat by the neck.

Acharon could see Sovelet struggling to keep her balance while pushing against the door. As he approached the dog began to shake Sovelet's sleeve more violently. She slipped and started to fall. The dog released her sleeve and then snapped up a different part, closer to Sovelet's hand.

"No!" Sovelet's voice was a mixture of demand and terror.

Acharon caught her under the arms as she continued to fall, stopping her from reaching the ground. He turned and put his back against the door and pushed. Sovelet fought against the dog's pull, her other arm grabbing at her sleeve as she leaned away from the door. Acharon unlatched his pistol holster and pulled the pistol free. He pointed it at the dog, hoping to scare it into retreat.

The dog barked and released Sovelet's jacket sleeve. She fell backwards and slid several feet. Before Acharon could act the dog twisted and bit the barrel of the pistol. Acharon yanked away from the dog. Its jaws held firm and Acharon's action against it put the final pressure needed to pull the trigger one sixteenth of an inch.

He hadn't expected the pistol to fire. When it did, he stepped back in surprise. The dog, with a large section of the back of its head missing, flopped to the ground. Behind it, the nearest dogs stumbled and fumbled back several yards, creating a half-circle of open space.

"The door."

He blinked hard and looked at the dog, its blood a growing island of red, and over to Sovelet.

"The door!"

Acharon holstered the pistol. The other dogs, still too fearful or unsure of what had happened, kept their distance. Acharon took advantage of the space and pulled the door open enough to push the dog out of the doorway with his boot. The dog was big and it took several hard pushes to get it far enough that Acharon could then use the door to shove it away.

As he was turning the locks he noticed the pack of dogs separating over to one side. They cleared a path that was quickly filled by the alpha dog. It stopped, standing over the body of the dead dog. It sniffed the busted skull and the body of the dog before turning to look at Acharon.

Its lips curled back as it growled. The growl grew deeper as it took two stiff-legged steps toward Acharon. The growl burst into a series of heavy barks. It barked the same way again. The third time the other dogs joined in. A ragged mob chorus of barks as all the dogs slowly closed the open space, shrouding the dead dog with their own bodies as they approached the glass wall.

The barking traveled like a wave, around the building. Dogs on all four sides barked and continued barking. The foyer buzzed with the angry energy.

Acharon stepped back and turned to find Sovelet close behind him.

"We should go," Sovelet whispered.

"We should. But where?"

"In there. For now." Sovelet indicated the square black column that housed the stairs and elevators. She tugged Acharon's arm and he turned to follow her.

All around them, the dogs continued barking furiously. The Alpha moving like a shadow just the other side of the glass, moving when Acharon moved. Its bark stood out for Acharon. A challenging bark.

He turned frequently to watch the alpha dog. He stumbled over his pack as he went to retrieve it. He fumbled with the straps, trying to pull it up and onto his shoulders. He grabbed the duffel bag second and looked around for Sovelet. A moment of panic set his heart racing at her absence.

"Ach, come on." She was holding the stairwell door open.

Acharon hurried toward her, the incessant barking of the dogs a soundtrack of defeat. He entered the stairwell as Sovelet ushered him through. He stopped and sank down to sit on the stairs.

"Did you see them?" he asked. "It was like they were mourning a fallen comrade. A soldier. And then the challenge."

Sovelet sat next to him on the stairs and pulled his hand into hers. She squeezed his hand and rubbed it as she spoke.

"Don't take it so hard, Ach. It's going to be okay. We can still get out of here."

"Can we? I don't know. They've got us penned in this time."

"What about the garage? There's got to be a garage, right?"

Acharon nodded, then snorted a derisive laugh. "Big, wide entrance. Splits two ways. If they're not already down there, they'll be there soon. And if we're caught down there…."

"We need to rest, Ach. Maybe there's some place upstairs with a couple couches or at least some comfy chairs. Let's rest and then think. Okay?"

Acharon nodded and pulled himself to his feet. "Right. Okay. A break."

He turned and looked up the stairwell before slowly taking the steps to the next landing, turning and continuing upward.

The first two floors were completely empty. They'd walked a circuit through each floor before continuing up. The third floor was more promising with some chairs and desks still in their offices.

"One more floor," Sovelet suggested.

The fourth floor turned out to be what they needed and more. They found four couches that they could pull into one room. They also found bottled water. They had no idea how old it was but knew that it would be a bit foul to drink.

"I can make a distiller," Acharon said. He latched onto the idea as a problem he could solve and set about rigging a system to evaporate and condense the water into their empty water bottles.

Acharon scavenged bits and pieces from other floors. Copper tubing from water fountains, plastic pipe from a storage room. An empty five-gallon water bottle that didn't smell particularly bad.

As he worked to assemble the still he could see that Sovelet had sat on one of the couches and removed her shoes and socks. She was watching him and he understood why. He'd almost lost it down in the foyer. She was worried. He'd been worried, too.

While working on the still he took short breaks to stand at the windows and look down. There were balconies on one angle of the building and he would peek over the rail and watch the dogs as they meandered around the building. Some lay on the road, resting or grooming. Others were involved in frolicking or mock fights. The one thing he could not see, and was glad for it, was the dog he'd killed.

It bothered him that he felt so much concern about not harming the dogs. It was clear they were trying to kill him and Sovelet. He should just blast them away with every round he had. A mental inventory checked his anger, reminding him that he really only had ten shotgun shells of serious ammo. The others, of which there were now sixteen, were just rock salt and rubber pellets. The handgun had one more clip of nine and five rounds still in it. At last rough count he saw forty or fifty dogs, but there were likely more. And they attacked as a pack. They weren't going to patiently wait for him to reload. No, they were going to tear him apart.

And still he resisted killing them. Was it because this was no longer humanity's world? Maybe he didn't have a right to destroy what was following in the wake of mankind's Last Wave. Let humanity leave nobly, without continuing the legacy of destruction that it had wrought upon the world and then upon itself.

All of that begged a simple question. Was he really willing to let himself and Sovelet die so as not to stain the final memories of humanity? He knew the answer, and it was no. He wasn't going to lie down and give up. He wasn't tired of waiting.

Acharon shifted the distillery he'd rigged so that it caught the last bands of sunlight peeking through the western buildings. He'd done all he could with his one and a half centuries of knowledge to maximize the output. It might work, it might not, but at least his brain had been given some distraction. It was just a matter of time.

He turned away, reflexively wiping his hands together. Sovelet was lying on the couch she'd claimed as her own. Her eyes were open but tired looking as she watched him.

"It ought to work," he said. He sat on the couch nearest where she reclined and began untying his boots. "We'll just have to wait and see."

"You should get some rest."

Acharon pulled off his boots and tossed them to the side. He wiggled his toes. It was hard to believe that only two days ago he'd been in the medi-pod. He could use an injection of whatever energy boost it was that the machine had given him. He hated feeling this tired. It made him feel useless.

"The dogs," he said. He lay back on the couch. He didn't recall wanting to do it, but it happened anyway. Then he realized Sovelet was helping. Or forcing him, if he was being honest. He acquiesced and found himself relaxing against the dusty couch cushions.

"I'll listen for the dogs," Sovelet said. "I'll wake you if I think they've gotten in the building. Rest, Ach. It's okay."

It wasn't okay. He wanted to tell her it wasn't, that he'd lied to her all these years. Things weren't okay because things were ending. And people like Murphy were ending early. He hadn't told her the truth about Murphy. He needed to but his mind wouldn't stay still. Just as he realized he was falling asleep, he fell asleep.

16

Acharon woke slowly to the sound of a keyboard. The click and clatter lacked rhythm. Maybe that was what stirred him from his dreams. Dreams that were a mixture of fear and comfort. Their island, safe, but filled with dogs. Dogs that barked and never stopped. But the keyboard noise scared the dogs and that seemed odd. And so he opened his eyes and wondered if he'd gone blind. Everything was dark.

He sat up and looked around. He saw light, pale, that highlighted the dark city, the odd street light still dotting the darkness. He'd slept through the night. Dawn was peeking over the horizon. He could have still been dreaming, he did still hear the clatter of a keyboard. But instead of the sound coming from everywhere, it was coming from his left. So he turned in that direction.

Sovelet sat on one of the other couches, more distant than the one she'd slept on. Her face and chest glowed with the light of a laptop screen reflecting off them. Her hands would move rapidly, the source of the keyboard clatter. They'd pause for a bit, there might be a slow and random series of key clicks, and then her fingers would begin racing across the keys once again.

Acharon, bursting with curiosity, waited until she paused and then cleared his throat.

"Oh!" Sovelet jerked back in surprise and then lunged forward to grab at the laptop that tilted forward on her lap and began to quickly slide off.

"Sorry," Acharon said. He noticed the power cord that wandered into the gloom of the unlit room. "You have a laptop."

Sovelet grinned. "I do. Took a bit of work and the guts of four others to get this one to do what I needed. But, yep, I got one."

"I'm curious what you're doing. But I'm more curious where you got it from."

"Put your boots on and I'll show you."

Sovelet shut the laptop down and grabbed Acharon's self-charging flashlight. She cranked on its handle while Acharon hurried into his boots and laced them up.

"And power," he said as an afterthought. "Where'd you get power?"

"Come see." She held out her hand.

Acharon rose with Sovelet's help and followed her to the stairwell, which was also where the power cord went. It actually turned out to be quite a few power cords, knotted and plugged together exactly as he'd taught her before. The cords wound their way upward and Sovelet headed in the same direction. Acharon followed.

"The dogs?" he asked.

"Still outside last I checked. Some have wandered into the underground parking as well. Most are asleep, noses tucked under their tails."

Acharon was pleased to see that Sovelet's spirits had improved during his nap. If only his spirits could catch up to hers.

They exited at the seventeenth floor, along with the power cords. The cords led off to the right and Sovelet followed the path without hesitation. She stopped outside a door. The power cord ran underneath the door and into the room.

"Don't freak out," Sovelet said. "I did."

"Freak out? Okay, I won't. I think."

"You probably won't," she said and smiled. She pushed the door open.

The light from the flashlight played across the room as Sovelet brought it to bear on a point near the back of the room. The light stopped on another couch. This one was already occupied. On it lay the mummified and partially decayed remains of a man. Acharon assumed it had been a man because of the double breasted suit that was now too big for the shriveled person in it.

"Um. Wow."

"I know," Sovelet said. She'd been stepping forward but looking frequently backward at Acharon. "I didn't see him at first. Scared me so bad I almost started to cry. Good thing all this was here to distract me."

"All this? All what?"

She handed Acharon the flashlight. "Look around."

Acharon turned the flashlight toward the rest of the room. He saw boxes. And he saw more boxes. Many of them were moving boxes and some of them were food supply boxes. Then there were boxes for computers and batteries and even ammunition. The boxes had been stacked to create walls, to create rooms.

"That's a bedroom over there," Sovelet said, pointing to a doorway in the boxes. "The kitchen is that way. But back here. Come see."

Acharon followed Sovelet around the body on the couch toward the building windows. There were several stainless steel boxes. They had LED lights glowing in an arc from red to green. Cables ran out the backs to other metal boxes that had thinner, flat cables that ran from them to the windows. The power cord that had led the way up to the room was plugged into the front of the stainless steel boxes.

"Solar windows?"

Sovelet nodded.

Solar windows had been hard to come by in the days of preparation. They'd been put to use in places that were high priority. Most of those happened to be on the East Coast, though Acharon had heard that there'd been some installed in the Los Angeles enclave. When the few remaining members of that enclave had taken the monorail to Tempe, Arizona, Acharon had suggested to Thyme and others that they go down to L.A. and retrieve the solar windows. Thyme had squashed the idea and no one wanted to annoy him at that time.

But here were four panels, all facing southward. They were high efficiency, and based on the fact that they and their equipment were still working, they were built to last.

"How did they get here?"

"Him, I imagine," Sovelet said. She went back to what was

probably the living room. "He must have had an ego. He kept a lot of stuff, articles and newspaper clippings, about himself. His dad was some sort of investor and he followed in his father's footsteps. He's a Last Waver, too. One of the firsts."

"And we never knew he was here." It was a statement of fact because they hadn't known. If Thyme had known he'd have sent his goons to haul the guy in. Or at least all his possessions. If you can't control the person, control the supplies they need.

Acharon wandered over to one of the boxes marked "ammunition."

"And I don't know how that was possible, either," Sovelet said. She was still standing and looking down at the deceased. "It seems he had his offices here from the beginning. As more and more of his friends and family died, he retreated more and more into this space."

"How did you draw that conclusion?"

Sovelet held up a book. "I didn't draw it. He left it all in journals. There's at least a hundred of them. Most of it is factual stuff, weather, people still alive, lists of supplies. Things you'd talk about. Anything but feelings and emotions."

"Thanks." Acharon was reading labels on boxes.

"The last pages, though, they're different." Sovelet flipped through the pages. "He starts questioning things. Life, really. The last page is, well, it's written the day he killed himself. It's not a suicide note. I don't think it is. He just writes a lot of stuff asking about what's the point of resisting? What reason is there for carrying on? He called it selfish. Then there's just blood."

"Sounds like he could have used a little time in a medi-pod. Have it print up some medications to deal with that depression." Acharon tried to sound flippant but he was thinking again of Murphy. He was thinking of the conversation that he and Sovelet had started to have at the automated diner. He needed a distraction.

"Anything else on this floor?" He asked.

Sovelet looked at him with a flat look that lasted a count of ten. Finally she shrugged and set the journal aside. "Yeah. All the offices are out there. It's weird. It's like everyone just went home for the day and they'll be back after the weekend or something."

Acharon grunted in response. He found something to distract him. He pulled out a pocketknife and began cutting open one of the boxes.

"Seriously," Sovelet said. She was staring in the direction where the offices would be. "Computers still on desks, calendars with appointments, family photos. And dead plants. Lots and lots of dead plants."

"That's too bad," Acharon said.

"For the plants?"

"For us," Acharon said. He held up an ammunition box. "Wrong size. Did you see a gun?"

"In his hand. There's blood and rotted flesh. It might not be good anymore."

"Probably not," Acharon said. "So you put together your laptop from the computers in the other offices?"

"No! That's the best part. He had a stack of laptops in boxes, sealed. Just like we'd have found at one of the supply warehouses. Some had problems so I had to sift through and then pick parts."

"And charge batteries with the solar windows."

"The batteries connected to the windows are on a trickle charge. They don't hold as much as they used to, but it was enough connect to a laptop. Luckily I was able to scrounge up all those extension cords. I felt like a regular Acharon with all my creative rigging."

She laughed and it made Acharon feel good inside.

"I saw that smile," she said.

"You did." He was digging through more boxes that had ammunition labels on them. "So what were you doing on your new toy."

She followed Acharon along the walls of boxes as he worked along, cutting tape and seals to examine the insides.

"Well, it took a while to get the computer running. Then I needed software that he didn't have. I don't think he had it. I wasn't going to tear open all the boxes. Eventually I got onto the Internet and was able to access some of the software on the servers. You have to love redundancy."

"You do," Acharon said. He was listening with half an ear. There were lots of boxes of ammunition for weapons he didn't have and couldn't find. The boxes that lined the walls and made up the walls weren't stacked by content, but seemed to have been placed wherever they built up the wall best. So far all he'd found that was relevant were boxes of ammunition for the handgun that was still in the dead man's hand. Unless he caught a break he'd have to seriously consider trying to clean it.

"So I was able to make contact with some of the others still out there, the gang in New York, Ines and Clara in Paris. Told them what we were up against."

"Did any of them have any useful suggestions?"

"They had some ideas. Some of them wouldn't work, but a couple of them I thought I could play with."

"No ideas for me?" He pulled a box that looked promising from a second row in the makeshift bedroom. It was oiled cardboard and had packing tape and straps banding it together. Its labeling was military in style and he had no clue what all the numbers and letters meant. It was too heavy to be rations. Acharon opened his pocketknife. He mentally crossed his fingers that the box was filled with handguns that took all the ammo he kept finding.

"They suggested you build a bridge to cross over the street."

"I'd need a torch and a crane."

"I told them you'd say something like that."

Acharon was looking for the tabs on the straps to pull them loose. "And for you they suggested?"

"Well, it was complicated. But I had a little help from the guys in Japan and Egypt. We had to hack into the services programs."

"Services programs?" The straps popped loose. He started slicing through the strapping tape.

"Yes, for the electrical, water, lights, street cleaners. Did you know the water still works on this floor?"

Acharon pulled the box lids open. "No I didn't. Street cleaners?"

"Yep. You're going to love this." She squeezed his arm to express her excitement. "We were able to program a street sweeper to go back online and it's going to come here! When it does, all we have to do is figure out how to get to it. But it's a start!"

Acharon grinned. "And these would be the finish."

"Grenades?" Sovelet took an involuntary step backward.

"No, too bad," Acharon said. "But these will work nearly as effectifely. They're stun grenades. When's the cleaner truck going to get here?"

"Not sure, honestly." She watched the box of stun grenades as Acharon lifted several of them out of their cardboard box. "I know it's on its way. Depends on charge and speed."

"If the lines under the streets are still working, it can charge while moving."

"Some of the lines have corroded. That's why I'm not sure on arrival time. I had to send it on a circuitous route to keep it on the charge lines. I figured we'd like it to have as full a charge as possible so we don't have to rely on the lines when we're in it."

"Then we have time."

"We do."

"Then we should start planning."

They returned downstairs with several boxes, including the stun grenades. They worked steadily until the sun was free of the horizon and charging toward its zenith. Around the time they were finishing their preparation they heard a rumble on Bush Street and the dogs began barking angrily. They both went to the windows to look.

One of the large street cleaners, capable of scrubbing the road with stiff bristled brushes, and then vacuuming it all up for disposal in a predetermined area, was working its way toward a spot directly in front of the building. When it stopped, the rumbling stopped. The only noise left was that of the dogs who were surrounding the cleaner, barking furiously at it.

Acharon studied the cleaner for several minutes, thinking about their plan.

"You know there isn't space for people in that thing."

"I didn't. I do now."

There was a cab area on the cleaner, but it was a closed white box. Since no human was ever intended to drive one, they didn't bother building in windows or even doors. Cameras and sensors ringed the entire outside of the vehicle, allowing it to work at an autonomous level within the confines of the street sensors. Except that Sovelet and her friends had made some adjustments for this cleaner. The cleaner was working off of gps coordinates from the remaining satellites and the last map of San Francisco, which was more than sixty years old.

Acharon pointed at the cleaner. "Right there, on the front. You see the ladder?"

"I see it," Sovelet said after a short pause. "Up, then?"

"Well, it's set to drive itself to where we need to go, yes?"

"That's the plan." She looked to Acharon as she spoke.

Acharon nodded and turned away from the windows. He started back to their preparation area. "Then let's hope we can make this work or we're going to be stuck on a little metal island in a sea of dangerous dogs."

Acharon capped water bottles from the seventeenth floor bathroom. His distillery had managed to clean seven ounces of water. He made some final adjustments to the rest of their equipment while Sovelet did things on the laptop. Acharon wasn't sure what all was happening on the computer when she was on it, but he never felt the need to ask. She was obviously good enough to bring them a lifeboat, so if she wanted to make one more entry on a chat log or blog site, she'd earned it in his eyes. He focused on rigging the stun grenades to his pack straps.

"Done," Sovelet said after a few more minutes. She shut the laptop with a solid click, unplugged it, and handed it to Acharon. "We're ready?"

Acharon slipped the laptop into the backpack. "As much as we're going to be. Still insist on carrying the duffel bag?"

"You know I can do it," she said. She hefted the duffel bag and slipped into the makeshift shoulder straps that Acharon had fashioned from a variety of tape, cloth, and metal clips he'd scavenged from the box-home upstairs.

"Then we're ready." Acharon pulled on the backpack. The stun grenades clanked and clunked against each other as he adjusted the straps. The pack was heavy, stuffed with Sovelet's laptop and as many of the grenades that he could find space for. The rest he carried in a basket he'd found upstairs.

They took their time on the stairs. They were both burdened with extra weight and didn't need to risk falling in foolish haste. When they got to the bottom and opened the door the sound of the dogs increased. The moment they stepped out into the glass-walled first floor they were noticed by several of the dogs. The barking aggression of the rest of the dogs was transferred from the quiet and motionless cleaner to the two humans. They rushed toward the glass. Their paws thudding against the windows like an out-of-sync drum corps.

Acharon watched them from a short distance back. He scanned them, looking for the Alpha. He didn't see the dog, but that didn't mean the dog wasn't there. He'd see it again, soon enough. He was sure of that.

Time to get to work.

"Here," he said to Sovelet. He handed her a packet of earplugs and goggles that he'd darkened the sides of with cardboard and tape. The earplugs would minimize the sound of the stun grenades and the tunnel-vision goggles would reduce the effect from the grenades when they exploded. "Get ready."

Acharon did the same, putting in earplugs and donning safety goggles. His goggles did not have the extra protection as he needed to be able to see any dogs coming in from the sides. When he was done he looked to Sovelet. She was slipping the goggles over her eyes and when they were set, she gave him thumbs up.

He nodded and headed to the door closest to Bush Street. There was a small bridge that led to the sidewalk, a pond filled with bracken and weeds underneath. At the door he pulled a wooden wedge from a pocket. It was the type used to hold doors open, but in this instance it was to keep a door from opening too far. He set it on the floor, just behind the door he was going to be opening.

He braced the doorjamb with his foot, checked to see that Sovelet was behind him, and turned the latch that retracted the lock.

The door slammed inward with the pressure of a dozen dogs behind it. It hit the wedge and the door slid an inch, then another, then finally stopped. The barking, despite the earplugs, was painfully loud. Paws and snouts pushed through the door. The door quivered with the energy transferred from the dogs to its hinges.

Acharon pulled on one of the stun grenades attached to a backpack strap. It came loose, leaving the safety pin behind. He tossed it over the highest dogs into the barking crowd just over its shoulders. Several dogs snapped at the grenade just as it exploded. The noise was louder than the dogs had been and the flash was bright even through closed eyes. The dogs weren't barking anymore.

He opened his eyes to see several dogs on the ground. The faces of two of them were bloody and burned. They would be out of commission for a while, which meant two fewer dogs to harass him and Sovelet.

Several more dogs looked exactly as the grenade intended. The dogs were stunned and it would take several minutes for them to recover. They were temporarily not a nuisance. The remainder of the dogs had hightailed it out of the area. Many had turned and were staring in a mixture of fear and surprise.

"Now, Sovie!"

Acharon pushed the door, kicked aside the wedge, and pulled it open again. Sovelet marched out before him and he moved close after her. As he stepped past the door he pulled two more stun grenades from the straps. When dogs started rushing toward them he threw one, then the other.

"Eyes!"

Sovelet covered her eyes with one hand but kept moving. There was a double whump of sound, air pressure, and bright light. Dogs yelped in a mixture of surprise and pain. None of them had been foolish enough to bite at the grenades this time. They were a third of the way to the cleaner.

"Clear," Acharon said.

Sovelet uncovered her eyes and continued to march toward the cleaning machine.

Acharon pulled two more grenades and threw them the moment the dogs moved again. He warned Sovelet, closed his eyes, and yanked two more grenades free. He had three more sets at the ready on his pack straps and two more sets hanging from the bottom of the pack as backup. They were over the little bridge and nearing the sidewalk.

Though a few of the dogs were still whimpering where they lay on the ground, the other dogs were becoming bolder. They edged forward, barking at the black tubes in Acharon's hands. When he tossed them toward the dogs, none of them attacked the grenades. Instead, those farthest from the tossed grenades charged Acharon and Sovelet, who were off the sidewalk and heading toward the front of the cleaner.

Acharon tossed two, one left, one right. He instantly grabbed two more while warning Sovelet and then tossed them front and back. There was the boom of the first two, a pause, and the boom of the second two. It blew a circle of open space between them and the dogs, except one. Somehow one had eluded the grenades and subsequent concussions. It was threatening Sovelet, who kicked at it while sliding sideways toward the ladder. Acharon saw what was happening and didn't hesitate. He pulled out his handgun and shot the ground near the dog's back paws.

The dog yelped as bits of the pavement kicked up, hitting his legs. It spun and stumbled around before retreating into the mass of dogs surrounding them. As before, the use of the handgun brought the rioting dogs to a standstill.

"Go, go, go," Acharon urged Sovelet. He pulled one grenade free while holstering the gun. He pulled a second grenade free and stood with his back to the ladder. Through the metal he felt the vibration of Sovelet's feet as she stomped her way to the top.

Around him the dogs were growling and barking, slowly closing a circle with Acharon at the center. He was sure they knew he was going to try to climb the ladder and couldn't throw more grenades than what he already had in hand. While the two grenades stopped some of the dogs the others could rush him while he tried to climb the ladder. But humans hadn't ruled the roost all those millennia for nothing.

"Incoming!"

Two grenades bounced onto the ground from above. Acharon tossed his toward the open spaces and then bound up the ladder. He lost his footing once when the grenades exploded like rolling thunder. He held on tight with his hands and quickly regained his footing and was at the top before the first dog was jumping at the bottom rungs.

"Nice throw," Acharon said. His breathing was labored as he fought to catch his breath. His whole body quivered with the rush of adrenaline.

"You, too," Sovelet said.

Acharon pulled his backpack off and fished out Sovelet's laptop. He handed it over and she had it open and was punching keys before he could even gain his feet.

"How long?" He had to shout to be heard over the dogs and through the earplugs.

"Trying to connect to the signal," Sovelet said. She was shouting, too. Then, "I got it. Okay, there it is."

She began to type furiously, the cacophony of barking forgotten in her mission. Acharon stood, his legs shaking with the residual fear from what they had done. He looked around, scanning the pack of dogs that seemed to have swelled to seventy or eighty. He was looking for just one. He found him not in the crowd of barking madness, but back by the door they'd come through to reach the cleaner.

The Alpha sat, its head in a quizzical tilt. Its eyes shifted from watching Acharon and Sovelet, then to the street cleaner, then back to Acharon. Acharon shuddered and turned away.

"Grab on," Sovelet yelled. She'd pulled the laptop onto her lap and had a hand wrapped around the base of an antenna.

Acharon sat and grabbed the top rung of the ladder. He nodded his head and said loudly, "Ready."

"And we're off!" Sovelet punched a few more keys.

The cleaner began to whine as its systems came online and the electrical engines revved up. A low scream began as the sweeper brushes started spinning. The jolt as the sweeper began was anticlimactic. Acharon barely felt the lurch as the sweeper rolled forward. He looked at Sovelet, who shrugged. Who knew?

17

It was a parade of madness in Acharon's opinion. The street cleaner truck was the drum major. It led a rabble of barking dogs down Market Street and then did a ragged right turn onto Fremont. The dogs leapt and barked at the cleaner. Several times there'd been a high-pitched yelp as one dog or another got too close to the sweeper discs and were struck by the unforgiving bristles.

"I went sailing once, down the coast," Acharon said. He had to continue to raise his voice to be heard over the thrum of the sweepers, the vacuum, and a pack of dogs now nearing a hundred in total. "A hundred-foot sailboat. Beautiful. At one point the ship was sailing along and a pod of dolphins were racing and jumping in the bow wave."

"You're comparing that to this?" Sovelet leaned close to Acharon as she spoke loudly but didn't shout.

Acharon caught her smirking at him. At least he hadn't regaled her with a retelling of the trip one more time.

"No. Contrasting it. Do you know the route the cleaner has to take?"

"Not exactly. It's got to avoid streets where there's blockage. Like the broken monorail on Market. I also directed it to keep to the center of streets and not attempt to clear a way through any barriers. So if a car's in the middle of the street it may turn around or back up or whatever it does and then find an open street."

Nothing the dogs could do surprised Acharon. If they'd come around a corner carrying a ladder, he wouldn't have even blinked in wonder. More likely, they'd look for high points to jump onto the street sweeper. Stay away from parked cars and anything else that might provide the dogs a jumping point. He scanned the area, looking for possible opportunities for them to attack from.

"Ach, relax and enjoy the cruise." She squeezed his arm which reflexively relaxed at her touch.

He wanted to laugh. He wanted to relax as well. But he'd been watching and he'd seen the Alpha several times. Always from a distance. It would watch the cleaner approaching and then dash off around a corner or through some weeds and bushes. It had happened as they'd turned onto Market, then again on Fremont, and as they'd turned onto Mission he'd seen the alpha dog watching from a block ahead. Only once was it not ahead and that was the turn onto Fremont when the dog had run left onto Fremont and the cleaner had gone right. After that, it hadn't been wrong about the direction the cleaner was heading.

That made Acharon uncomfortable. A lot of things were making him uncomfortable. Finding Murphy, finding Carter and Hillary in their recliners, finding Thyme, and then finding this other Last Waver they'd never met. All of them died alone. Four by their own hand. And Acharon had lied about one of those.

He moved over to where Sovelet sat cross-legged and plopped down beside her.

"Sovie, I have to tell you something." He found moving close to her ear when talking helped with the volume.

"We can't stop so you can go to the bathroom." She grinned.

Acharon didn't, and that stifled hers.

"So it's something serious, serious?" She asked.

"It's about Murphy," Acharon said. He paused while he prepared himself. "He didn't die of a heart attack or aneurysm, or anything like that."

"He killed himself."

Acharon nodded. He wasn't sure what to expect from Sovelet next. "He left a note. 'Sorry, got tired of waiting.'"

He watched her as her mind chewed on the information.

"Well, I'm not surprised. Not really."

"You're not?"

"He'd been fading for years," Sovelet said. "Remember when he arrived? He'd spent two years traveling all over the country, visiting other enclaves. Remember how full of life and energy he'd been? Then he'd moved over to Sausalito with us. But when he got his own house and just stayed there, he got smaller and smaller."

"Smaller?" Murphy had been halfway between six and seven feet.

"Psychologically, mentally. He was slowly disappearing. Frankly, I'm surprised he waited so long."

"Oh," said Acharon, because he didn't know what to add to the conversation.

"You want to know what I don't know?"

"Yes." Though with trepidation.

Sovelet turned to face him. She had to raise her voice over the background noise as she looked him straight in the eyes. "Why didn't you tell me the truth?"

"Because you were sick," he said. "Because I know how you think, and how you'd been thinking of late. I was afraid that if you heard he'd taken his life you might feel inclined to let yourself go."

"I might have," Sovelet said. "I'd already been thinking about it. You know that, too. We weren't doing anything anyways. So what was the point?"

"The point? The point is that we're alive and we shouldn't go and waste that."

"But we are," Sovelet said. She placed a hand on Acharon's knee, gave it a squeeze. "We're not staying alive for the grandkids. Nor for family and friends or even anyone else that might look to us for inspiration or comfort. We're it, Ach, and whether we live a long or short life, it doesn't matter. There's no one here to judge us. There's no one here that needs us."

"You sound like someone from one of the suicide cults," Acharon said. "Besides, I need you."

She squeezed his knee again and then patted it. "I know and I wouldn't want to lose you, either. Because I need you, too. I just think we need to reevaluate how we live."

Before Acharon could respond, movement at the front of the street cleaner drew his attention away. He looked up to see a dog grasping the top rung of the ladder with its teeth. Its front paws searching for purchase, some way to secure itself so it could climb onto the top of the cleaner.

"We definitely need to reevaluate how we're living today," Acharon said.

He got up and walked toward the dog. It had gotten one paw hooked around the rung where its teeth had been. It was now barking and snapping at Acharon. Acharon waited, timing the dog's movements. When it finished a bark he kicked it under the jaw. The dog toppled backwards and hit the ground with a yelp. The cleaner continued moving forward and the dog scrambled to its feet and limped off, favoring its front left paw.

Acharon's actions caused another outburst among the dogs who jumped and barked more furiously than before.

He took the time to look forward. They'd passed over Main Street and were approaching Spear Street. In the middle of the cross street sat the Alpha. It watched Acharon, its head tilted to one side, as the sea of dogs and the cleaner they surrounded slowly approached. When the cleaner was a hundred feet away, the Alpha got up and trotted down Spear without a single look back. As the cleaner crossed Spear, Acharon saw the Alpha break into a run and disappear around the corner on the next block.

Acharon would give almost anything to know what was going through the alpha dog's mind.

He walked a cautious perimeter along the top of the cleaner. It was a well-built machine. Even after decades of sitting idle, it still moved smoothly on the road. There wasn't any wobbling or jerking as it whipped the dirt from the road and sucked it up with its vacuum.

Down near the ground, dogs at various points around the vehicle were attempting the same thing as the dog he'd just given the boot. Some would leap up, grab at any protuberance with their jaws or scrabbled at the surface with their claws, all before slipping and falling away from the cleaner. Several times a dog managed to hold on for an extra amount of time and several had made it halfway up the slight slope of the back before tumbling down into the crowd of dogs jumping and leaping behind the cleaner.

They were getting more ambitious.

He went and stood by Sovelet, scanning the front edge of the cleaner and the streets around them. Sovelet stood, steadying herself against him.

"I didn't mean today," she said. "Nor yesterday. These last couple of days are definitely outliers."

"Yeah, I could definitely live without the last few days."

Sovelet hugged his arm with hers and squeezed. "Except we're living."

"You like this?" Acharon looked at her, unconsciously kissing the top of her head. Behind her he saw the nose of dog peek above the side of the cleaner and then disappear with a yelp. "We've been chased, bitten at, harassed. Both of us could have died anywhere along the way."

"No. No I don't like this, Ach." She stepped in front of him and wrapped her arms around him, squeezing tightly enough that he hugged her back in response. She looked up the short distance their height difference required. "But at least we're doing something with our lives."

"We were doing something with our lives on the island."

"What? Exactly?" Her raised eyebrows added challenge to the question.

What, exactly? Acharon paused. They'd spent thirty years on the island. They'd worked to make it a comfortable and safe place to live out the rest of their lives.

"Living," he said. The answer felt lame even to him.

"Not living." She hugged him again. "We were just existing. Doing what Murphy was doing, what that man in the high-rise was doing. We just had company."

"What were they doing?"

There was an uptick in noise coming from the front of the cleaner but Sovelet held him in place.

"Murphy's note: Got tired of waiting. That's all we're doing. We're waiting, we're just doing it more comfortably than Murphy did, than the other man did. And we're waiting for nothing."

Acharon heard more scrabbling from the front of the cleaner.

Looking up he could see that they were almost to the Embarcadero. He slowly freed himself from Sovelet's hug and picked up the shotgun.

"What do you suggest?" he asked as he walked toward the front of the cleaner. The noise in the front was louder. This time he led with the shotgun.

As Acharon neared the front of the cleaner, two dogs scrabbled over the edge. Their front legs were splayed out in front, their chests heaving with the effort. Behind them several other dogs were supporting them with their heads. Behind them, several more supported them. It was a circus pyramid of dogs.

The two dogs looked up to see Acharon approaching. One of them wriggled, its eyes showing panic, and slipped off the roof. The second barked furiously at Acharon who responded with a round of rock salt.

The dog yelped as the blast of rock salt knocked its front paws off the roof, sending the dog backwards onto the dogs below. Acharon continued to the edge and looked down. Half a dozen dogs were still clinging to the front of the cleaner, several of them holding on with their teeth. More dogs were scrambling over their backs, scratching bloody lines into those they passed over. Dogs that slipped and fell quickly scrambled to avoid the stiff and uncompromising bristles of the spinning brushes.

"Cover your ears," Acharon said. He pulled a stun grenade from his jacket pocket. He rested the shotgun in the crook of his arm while he pulled the pin, let the spoon fly, and let the grenade roll down to the dogs. He turned and started walking away when the grenade went off.

The concussion from the explosion knocked Acharon to his knees. He automatically put his hands out to catch himself and his shotgun bounced loose. He lunged for it but it was too late. The shotgun dropped over the side.

"Dammit!" He'd leaned too far over the edge. He almost had his balance back when he locked eyes with the Alpha sitting amongst a small grove of young palm trees. He had one hand pushed against the side of the street cleaner. He kept trying to lean back, right himself. It wasn't working. What was worse, his pack was slowly sliding forward, higher on his shoulders. It was throwing off his balance more with each inch it moved. Below, dogs jumped and snapped furiously at his face and hand. He wasn't going to make it.

"Sovie!"

The pack stopped moving on his back. He could feel it slide back into position and he was slowly tipping back onto the roof of the cleaner. He looked over his shoulder once he was completely on the roof. Sovelet sat behind him, her hands still on the straps stitched to the bottom of the pack.

"Are you okay?" Sovelet asked.

Acharon slapped the roof with an open hand. It hurt but he did it again.

"Well, I lost the shotgun."

"I'm sorry," Sovelet said. She squeezed his calf.

"Me, too. And they aren't going to be completely happy, either. Now all I have is the pistol. It doesn't shoot salt. No more mister nice guy."

They both pushed back to the center of the roof. The stun grenade seemed to have taken some of the adventure out of the dogs. Acharon didn't hear any more of them attempting to climb the cleaner as it turned onto the Embarcadero. They were almost to the warehouse.

"You asked what I would suggest."

"I did?"

"You did," Sovelet said. "Just before the dogs distracted you."

"Before I lost the shotgun."

"Don't beat yourself up over that. Anyway, I think we should live life, not just wait for the end of it. Look at today. If things went wrong and we died here today, at least we were living our lives. Being active. Not just sitting on our rocking chairs on our wonderful little island, waiting for the end."

"So you want to live like this? Fight every day for the right to be alive?"

Sovelet laughed. "Definitely not this. But something more than what we already have."

"What?" Acharon turned to her as he asked. He'd thought she wanted nothing more than to live comfortably the rest of their days. To grow old together and hopefully die together. But not in violence, not by their own hand. While sleeping in bed is how he'd always imagined it would be. And they would be the last people to go to sleep on the Earth and the last people to leave it.

"Well, that depends on things. Computer things. I'll give you a straight answer after I get onto the computers in the warehouse."

"If we get there," Acharon said. He'd lost the shotgun. The number of dogs seemed to be growing.

And when it felt like he was going to fall off the cleaner, he'd seen the alpha dog start to hurry forward. He was glad to be a disappointment to it, but he didn't like being disappointed in himself.

"We'll get there," Sovelet said. She stroked the side of his face several times. He leaned into the caress. "Rest a bit. While you can. While we can."

Acharon barked a short laugh of pessimism, then softened his reaction with a kiss to her cheek.

There was little time to relax. The further along the Embarcadero they moved, the more frantic and determined the dogs seemed to become. There was also the number of dogs to consider as well. There were too many, moving too quickly, jumping and leaping at the sides of the cleaner for Acharon to count exactly. He was pretty sure, however, that the number had swelled to something well over a hundred. A hundred-plus angry, barking, determined dogs. All he had in defense was a clip and a half for the handgun and eight stun grenades.

He tried to relax, to sit down and just feel the sun on his face, smell the bay water that was much fresher than when he was a boy. If he closed his eyes and blocked out the sound of more than a hundred dogs barking incessantly, he could almost pretend they were on their island, free of all the stress and danger. But then he'd hear the scrabbling of a dog nearing the roof of the cleaner and he'd be back in the reality, sliding across the roof to kick another dog loose, sending it flailing back into the seething crowd of canines.

As the hour rolled by and the sun tipped west over its zenith, Acharon shoved seven dogs off the cleaner and tossed two stun grenades into the pack of dogs. He made sure to stay low when the grenades exploded. He didn't want to lose anything else, especially himself. When the opportunity presented itself, he would stand up and scan the road before them, behind them. He also kept an eye on the trees and bushes to their left. He'd seen the Alpha when they'd approached pier Nine. The Alpha sat among trees a half block ahead and quickly disappeared as the cleaner approached.

Now, as Acharon gave the boot to two more dogs, the eighth and ninth since turning onto the Embarcadero, he stood to stretch. Ahead, he saw the warehouse. Pier Twenty-three, the Last Wave warehouse, was just ahead. Then he realized the gate was open. He was pretty sure he'd closed it when they'd left in the Jeep. That was just a few days ago, but felt like forever.

Fortunately, it had opened only a couple of feet. It had probably rolled open, he decided. When he'd closed the gate there'd probably been mounded dirt and the wheels had slowly rolled off over the last few days. On one hand, he didn't like that the gate was open. On the other hand, perhaps it was a good thing that it was open.

"Sovie? Where's the cleaner supposed to stop at?"

Sovelet looked up from her computer, which had been occupying her full attention once she'd picked up a useful wifi signal. She seemed surprised by their location.

"Oh! Just a moment," she said. She tapped her fingers across the keyboard, paused, then nodded. "It should stop just short of the gate. There's enough satellites still operating that the precision should be pretty close to dead accurate."

"Could you make it stop parallel to the fence?"

Sovelet studied the screen of the laptop. "Yes."

"Can you make it stop right against the fence?"

She shook her head. "If I could reach two more satellites, yes. Best I can do is a meter, plus or minus a half meter."

"We'll make it work."

Acharon looked over at the warehouse. Now that they were within sight of it, the distance seemed to be closing faster. He needed to move quickly. He slipped off the pack and began unhooking the last of the stun grenades. He slipped two into his pockets and then tied the others to antennae bases and the top rung of the ladder. He paused long enough to kick another dog off the edge of the roof.

"I'm going to need your help, Sovie."

Sovelet closed her laptop and scooted across the roof. She pulled the goggles back over her eyes. "What do you need me to do?"

"We need to keep the dogs from entering the warehouse's courtyard. I think we can use the grenades to scare them away from the front of the cleaner. At the last moment, one to each side of the front. We slide down the ladder, cross to the fence, and pull the gate closed behind us. Keep one last grenade with you in case they try to rush the gate before I get it closed. All right?"

Sovelet nodded and put her hand on one of the grenades tied to the cleaner roof. Acharon smiled and slid over to the ladder. This was their last gambit. They had everything to lose if they didn't pull it off.

He watched as the cleaner moved closer and closer to the gate of the warehouse courtyard. They were still on the Embarcadero. The warehouse was at a slight bend in the Embarcadero so the dogs might not catch on until it was too late. They might not catch on at all, he reminded himself. If only he hadn't noticed the alpha dog watching them all morning, he might have more easily convinced himself that the dogs weren't capable of catching on to the plan.

The time for wishing, though, had come to an end. Acharon pulled the pin on the first stun grenade and lobbed it toward the outer edge of the dogs in front. The dogs edged away as the grenade hit the ground near them. Acharon held the ladder rung and braced himself as the grenade exploded. There was the flash and bang and a chorus of yelping as the grenade did its job. Acharon looked up after the flash and saw that the dogs had been pushed to the sides. He tossed the second grenade.

The second explosion pushed the dogs back further. They moved to the sides, barking and biting at the cleaner.

Acharon tossed the third grenade.

"Get ready," he said. He stepped down onto the ladder, a fourth grenade in his free hand.

Sovelet grabbed her two grenades and pulled them free, leaving the safety pins behind.

The third grenade exploded just as the cleaner made a slight adjustment to the right. The dogs moved further aside. The cleaner rocked as it crossed onto the sidewalk.

Acharon dropped the fourth grenade just as the cleaner slowed at the fence gate. He waited until the sound and flash faded and looked around him. The cleaner had stopped. Fortune was finally on his side. They were less than a meter from the fence. They only had to climb down, take two steps to the right, and two steps through the gate.

"Now," he shouted. He jumped from the ladder and hit the ground, stumbling. He held his forearm over his eyes as Sovelet's grenades exploded to either side of the cleaner. His pack thumped down beside him. Sovelet followed.

"I'm down," she said.

"Go!" He pushed her toward the open gate, grabbing his pack as they moved past it.

They were stepping through the gap when the dogs recovered and began to rush into the open space. Acharon dropped the last grenade and closed his eyes as he pulled on the gate. The explosion, so close, warmed his skin and staggered him with the concussion. He managed to retain his grip on the fence, straining to bring the gate into contact with the fence.

The latch clicked into place. Acharon let go and opened his eyes. They'd done it.

Inches away, on the other side of the fence, the dogs jumped and barked. Some of them bit at the chain link, worrying at it. Let them, Acharon thought. They'll be at it long after he and Sovelet were away from the city.

He was grabbed from behind. Sovelet hugged him furiously. "We did it!"

"Not yet. Not quite," Acharon said. He pulled away from Sovelet and snatched up the backpack. "Not until we're inside the warehouse."

He grabbed Sovelet's hand and turned to the door and stopped. The alpha dog was standing in front of the door. Its lips were pulled back, baring long and shiny-wet canines. A low throaty growl could be heard over the barking dogs, barking dogs that were slowly ceasing their frenetic activities as they focused on what was happening inside the fence.

"Ach?"

"The roll-up door. Move that way."

Acharon stepped back, pushing Sovelet behind him, and edged sideways.

The Alpha took several short steps forward, keeping itself between Acharon and the door that Sovelet had used the day they'd arrived at the warehouse.

Acharon moved slowly but purposefully, shielding Sovelet. He guided them to the roll-up door, to the edge where the chain hung.

"Can you pull on that?" He asked Sovelet.

"I can. I think."

"You just have to get it high enough for us to slip under. Put your weight on it, it should come."

Acharon kept his eyes focused on the dog. Behind him he could hear the rattle of chain. The Alpha lunged forward but jumped back when Acharon pulled his handgun from its holster.

"Try it," he said to the dog. "Try it."

The Alpha barked a rapid succession of barks but remained where it was. Its eyes shifted to watch Acharon and then the chain that Sovelet was pulling.

The gate rose slowly, click-clacking its way upward.

Time felt as if it had frozen for Acharon. He could have been standing there for minutes or hours. Only when the sound of the chain grinding against the geared pulley overhead stopped did he feel like time had started once again.

"I think it's up enough," Sovelet said. "I hope."

Acharon turned his head just enough to see the roll-up and keep the Alpha in his sights. It looked like enough. He hoped it was enough.

"Get under," he said. "Then grab the chain on the other side. Get ready to pull the door down when I come under.

"Ach." Her voice was full of worry.

"I'll be fine," he said. "Just get ready."

"Okay." He heard Sovelet scraping her way under the door. She paused. "I love you, Ach."

"I love you, too, Sovie. Go."

The Alpha was growling louder, moving sideways. Acharon turned and stepped sideways to keep the dog from trying to gain access to the gap below the roll-up. The absolute last thing he needed was for Sovelet to be trapped inside with the dog.

"Ready!" Her voice sounded distant, vibrating with the echo of the large empty chamber.

Acharon pushed the pack through the gap with one foot. He slowly knelt and then lay on his side. All the while he kept the gun trained on the alpha dog. He had to get under and then keep low so that he could keep an eye on the dog. Slowly he slid under. The Alpha growled louder. Saliva dribbled in long strings from its mouth. Every muscle in its body seemed tense and bunched.

Acharon pushed and slid below the roll-up. He lost sight of the dog for just a second and that was all the dog required.

Acharon's leg stopped moving. There was pain as his leg was suddenly jerked back into the courtyard. There was a brief moment where it felt as if he'd shaken it free and then the pain went through the roof as pointed teeth clamped onto his calf. He yelled in anger and surprise as he found himself sliding further back from where he'd tried to leave. He grabbed at the roll-up but the pain in his leg affected his focus and his grip and he found himself suddenly back in the courtyard, on his back, and the alpha dog lunging at his throat.

He threw his arm up to block the attack. The dog's teeth sank into his arm and he grunted with the pain. The dog shook his arm, tearing the skin and flesh.

The pain was worse than the mountain lion, the fear greater. This time there wasn't a mysterious shotgun booby trap to save him. He was on his own this time. But he had a gun. Where was it? He had it, in his hand, ready to fire.

Somewhere he could hear Sovelet screaming. Was there another dog?

Acharon became angry as well as frightened. He had not pushed and fought to get this far to lose her. Especially not like this. Not living like this. He pulled the trigger on the handgun. He heard the report as the gunpowder exploded. The dog remained unfazed, yanking and tearing at his arm. A moment of focus showed the problem. The gun was in the hand of the arm being mauled by the dog. It took a Herculean effort to convince his hand to release the gun, but finally his fingers opened and the gun dropped.

He grabbed it with his other hand and shoved the end of the barrel into the ribs of the dog and pulled the trigger. The dog yelped and started to release Acharon's arm. Acharon pulled the trigger again and the dog collapsed on him, dead.

The world went silent and Acharon wondered if he'd gone deaf from the gun being so close to his ears when he'd pulled the trigger. But as he moved he heard the scrape of his clothes against the concrete, the clink of the handgun as he set it aside. He could hear, but everything was still quiet. Where was the incessant barking of the dogs?

He pushed the dog off him and sat up. He sucked air between clenched teeth with every move. His leg throbbed with pain and his arm fairly screamed of its own accord. Beyond the chain link fence the other dogs still stood. They looked on in silence. Acharon looked around at them and then down at the Alpha, one side of its chest a bloody mess. Its blood pooled around them both, soaking into Acharon's pants. He felt guilty.

He was not sorry that he'd defended himself, that he chose to live. Yet, the death of the dog left him feeling a sense of guilt. Here they were, one species descending, the other ascending, and the former couldn't just go peacefully. No, it seemed that it had to go kicking and screaming into the night with all the violence it had wrought upon the world. The other, intent on finding its place in the new order, challenging the past to claim its right to the future.

With a shaky hand and a pain-screaming arm, Acharon reached out and stroked the dog. In another time, he might have been a companion rather than the enemy.

Acharon heard a noise and looked up. A dog had shaken its head, making its ears flap against its head. It was turning away to leave. All of the dogs, or those that still remained, were also leaving. They left, not as a pack, but as a dispersed crowd. Acharon considered the Alpha. Perhaps he'd been the first attempt at the advancement of the canine species. Perhaps there would be others.

The thought of others reminded him of Sovelet.

He'd heard her screaming. He'd thought there was another dog. He reached out to pick up the handgun and noticed all the blood. Two pools of blood, slightly different in color, spreading toward each other. The past and the present, mingling. And he was so tired and he wondered if maybe he was tired of waiting. Or was he just sleepy tired? But he had Sovelet to think of. He tried to move. He heard the sound of metal behind him. And then there was nothing to worry about anymore.

18

Acharon woke to clear plastic and sterile light. The air lacked smell, which meant that it was being recycled and filtered. He'd been asleep. No, unconscious seemed the more likely answer. Something had woken him. He couldn't recall what it was. He wasn't sure how he'd gotten where he was. He tried to move and clarity clawed his body.

He ached, seemingly everywhere. His leg and his arm pulsed with discomfort that was barely manageable. Overhead, something whirred and moved. Acharon squinted, trying to focus on the movement through the plain white light. A metal arm had swung out from somewhere behind him. He recognized it as a hypodermic arm. Its needle end disappeared from view. He felt a pinch. The pain in his body retreated to the edges of his consciousness.

Acharon sighed with the relief.

He heard a tapping noise and slowly turned his head. There was pain there, too, but it was slowly fading. More than an arm's length away, Sovelet was standing outside the medi-pod. She waved and then waited as the door slowly rose up and out of the way. She poked her head through the opening when it was high enough.

"Feeling better?"

"Depends."

Sovelet stepped into the medi-pod. She held his hand and gave it a gentle squeeze.

"What does that mean, 'depends'?"

"Are we back to square one?" He looked around but the bright light in the medi-pod made it difficult to see beyond the plastic bubble. "Are we at the medi-fac again?"

Sovelet smiled. "No."

"Promise me, then, that this isn't the enclave."

"I promise."

"Where are we?"

"The warehouse," she said. "The medi-pod. You don't remember coming in here?"

Acharon sifted through his memories, trying to recall what had happened last. It should have been lying down on the medi-pod table. But it wasn't. The last memory was lying down in a pool of blood and thinking that he was glad it was over.

"I remember the dog. The dogs leaving. Blood. I think I heard the door rolling up again."

"That was me," Sovelet said. Her face kept shifting up to happiness and down to concern. "I thought I was going to have to drag you all the way here. But you stood. Sort of. And then kept apologizing for killing the dog the entire time we staggered into here and I got you to lie on the table. You're heavy."

"Even after losing all that blood?"

She kissed him on the nose. "Even after. You think you can sit up?"

With her help, Acharon slowly moved to a sitting position. The pain wasn't as bad now, but there was still pain. And he felt weak, exhausted.

"I heard you scream? When the Alpha attacked me. I thought there was a second dog."

"There was just the one," she answered. She held out an open shirt and helped him slide into it. The plastic skin on his right arm went from wrist to elbow and all the way around. A lot of plastic skin meant a lot of damage. He flexed his arm to make sure it still worked.

"I screamed because I thought I'd lost you." She patted his chest after slipping the last button through its hole.

"I thought I'd lost you. And me."

"Well, we both survived. Admittedly you could be a lot better. This medi-pod is an older version. It could fix the internal stuff and restitch the bone, but it doesn't have the newer skin printers, just the plastic stuff. More bandage than skin. You're gonna have scars."

Sovelet knelt to help him get his legs into new pants. His leg was crisscrossed with angry red lines, ghostly visible through the plastic skin. Lines that showed where the dog had torn into his leg. He flexed his foot. It hurt, but it worked.

"Wait. Restitch bone?"

Sovelet put her hand on his leg. It was soft and warm and made Acharon feel safer.

"It cracked your fibula." She stepped back and held out a hand. "Come to the office. There's a couch. And food."

Gingerly, Acharon shifted himself off the table and onto his feet. When he'd had his eye printed and installed he'd left the medi-pod as fit as before the attack. This time he still felt beat up. He leaned against the table to rest a moment. The floor was cold against the bottoms of his bare feet.

With a smile and an assist from Sovelet he managed to move out of the medi-pod and then out of the mobile clinic. The more he walked the better his battered body began to feel. It didn't hurt that he was motivated by food and a desire to get his feet off the cold cement.

Sovelet stayed by his side, her hand hovering by his elbow. She stayed that way until he'd navigated his way up the even colder metal stairs and into the office where he gratefully, but slowly, sat on the couch.

"One shouldn't feel so tired after spending time in a medi-pod," he said. The medi-pod at the enclave had been thoughtful enough to give him an energy boost. But it had also been top of the line. "I feel like I've been playing football for a week, nonstop."

"Here, this will help." She brought Acharon a steaming bowl of reconstituted vegetable stew and a tube of sourdough bread.

"There's food here, too?"

"Several containers full. Still in good shape. Eat."

Acharon dug in, balancing the tray with stew and bread on his knees while he ate. The stew was hot and satisfying, especially when soaked up in the bread. He sipped and chewed and made appreciative noises while Sovelet watched and silently waited.

"Better?" Sovelet asked as Acharon scrapped the last drops of stew off the bowl with a piece of bread.

"Yes, I am, thanks." He set the bowl on the floor and chewed on the last piece of bread. "I'm just not used to feeling so tired, so beat up after getting out of a medi-pod."

He slouched back on the couch. His left hand rubbed softly on the aching wounds of the right arm.

"Imagine a time when they didn't have medi-pods."

"Imagine a world full of people where dogs followed them to get treats and a pat on the head."

"They all left," Sovelet said. She looked in the direction of the Embarcadero even though several walls blocked the view. "When you killed-- when the dog died, they just left."

"I can't even pretend to understand. Perhaps it was his idea. He was the first to see us arrive. Maybe this was all his doing and like some tribal warrior, he had to prove his right to lead, which meant keeping us from leaving. He took the final challenge on himself."

"And paid for it."

Acharon nodded. "I doubt they have a memory of humans and certainly not how violent we can be. I didn't want to kill him, but I didn't want to die, either."

"Well, I'm glad you didn't."

"I'm glad I didn't, either." The feeling of being weak from blood loss and the pain of his wounds were clarifying themselves the longer he was awake. "I thought I was going to."

"You didn't. You're here." She stood. "And now I want to show you something."

She helped to haul Acharon to his feet. He let her put more work into it than necessary, enjoying the help.

"What are you going to show me?"

She guided him over to a computer terminal. She gently pushed him onto the seat and then leaned over him. She attacked the keyboard with her fingertips. Several aggressive seconds later, a map of the United States appeared. A bright red line, starting in the San Francisco Bay, zigged and zagged across the country, finally ending about halfway up the East Coast.

"This is?"

"This," Sovelet said and touched the red line on the screen, "is a workable route to New York from Oakland. I started testing the monorail lines while I was waiting for you to make the Jeep."

"That what you were doing at the medi-fac and the high-rise? Both times while I was asleep, I'll remind you."

She hugged him from the side. "And when we stopped at the rest station, too. I'd set up a program to test each viable section of rail and have it find connections to New York."

"You haven't forgotten that we already have a home here? Or does this have something to do with living and not waiting."

"It does. There's twenty people gathered in New York. We'd have a community again. They aren't like Thyme and his hoodlums. There's lots of space on Manhattan Island. The museums are remarkably preserved. They're even talking about going to Europe. To Paris."

"The ships aren't running anymore."

Sovelet poked some keyboard keys and made pictures of an old shipyard come up on the screen. Several men and women about the same age as Acharon and Sovelet were standing by a wooden boat shell. They were grinning.

"They're building it. Seventy feet."

Acharon studied the image, focusing mostly on the boat. "It's got nice lines."

"And you do love to sail."

"I do love to sail," Acharon said. He looked at the picture. Friendly people. People with a purpose and a new ship to sail. It would be different. "Do we need to go back to the island for anything?"

She took his hand in hers. "Do you need anything from there?"

"I have everything I need right here."

"Is that a subtle way of saying you agree to my idea?"

"Are you kidding? After the way this week has gone?" He took her hand and kissed it. Grateful to have her as his lifelong companion. "I could use a vacation."

The End

ABOUT THE AUTHOR

Earl T. Roske is a San Francisco Bay Area writer who juggles writing with childcare, housecleaning, cooking, and dog walking. Despite all that, he still continues to not only write, but to enjoy the process as well.

If you enjoyed this book, consider leaving a review online. It helps readers choose a book and it helps the author, too.

If you're interested in new work by the author, or just want to drop him a line, try the following.

Follow on Facebook:
www.facebook.com/EarlTRoske/

Follow on Amazon to be notified of future releases:
www.amazon.com/Earl-T.-Roske/e/B006GD53XE

Follow on Twitter:
twitter.com/earltroske

And, of course:
www.earltroske.com

Finally:
earltroske@earltroske.com